# REDEEM ME

A. LONERGAN

NIGHT SHADE PRESS, LLC

Copyright © 2021 by A. Lonergan

All rights reserved.

No part of this book may be reproduced in any form or by any electronic or mechanical means, including information storage and retrieval systems, without written permission from the author, except for the use of brief quotations in a book review.

*To the ones that fought or are fighting for redemption. You are never too far or too lost for it. This is for you.*

## CHAPTER 1
RAFE CRIMSON

The night replayed on a loop in my head. Everywhere I looked I saw Jade. I saw her broody looks and the little smiles she threw at my Guardians. I saw her green eyes in my dreams and when I woke up, she was still gone. No matter what I wanted to do, my hands were tied. I went over the night in my head again. I couldn't stop it.

*"She's gone," Mav shouted down our pack bond.*

*"Who?" I knew before his voice vibrated through my head.*

*"Jade!"*

*A roaring filled my ears. "Where is she?"*

*It was Knox that answered this time. "We aren't sure. We have Pack Police on the scene but it doesn't look good."* *Even in my head he sounded strained. "It smells like rogues.*

*Their scent is always off, but then it doesn't. The wind will blow and another scent will replace it."*

*Witches. The witches were meddling again. That was the only way to explain it. "How much damage?"*

*Archer sighed. "I don't think rogues did this."*

*I hopped on my motorcycle and kicked it to life. I didn't have time to listen to this in my head. I didn't know why I had waited so long to get there. I should have hopped on my bike immediately. I wasted enough time.*

*When I got to the scene my stomach dropped. Tracey's SUV was upside down and the windows were busted out. No airbags had been deployed. Blood splattered on the light leather seats and my stomach clenched. Where was the car that had hit them? Was it a car that hit them? Based on the massive dent in the side of the car and all the damage, it had to be a big truck. I scratched my jaw and sniffed the air.*

*Knox had been right. The wind shifted and took the rogue scent away then there was nothing. With every breeze it was a different scent. We would be going in circles if we followed that.*

*Archer was at my side in seconds. Knox was still looking over Tracey's SUV and Mav had his head in his hands. Tracey was seated on the edge of a stretcher with an ice pack pressed to her bleeding forehead. Both of her eyes were black and her arm was in a sling. With the wolfsbane in her system, she would be healing slowly.*

*"Who saw what happened?" My voice didn't sound like my own. It didn't even sound like my wolf had taken over.*

*Mav's eyes rose up to meet mine. They were bloodshot and haunted. "The light was taking too long to change. We knew something wasn't right. I saw the truck hit them. We tried to get there, but we were too far. I jumped out of the car, but I wasn't fast enough. We were too far away. I failed you, Alpha." Damn wolfsbane needed to be banned. We shouldn't have been drinking tonight. We should have known the threat was too great, even if it did smell like rogues.*

It was too organized to be rogues. Rogues were crazy. This was all a setup to make it look like it had been them. Everything was too planned out for a random attack. This was a bigger game, a bigger ploy. One I needed to figure out before my mate was killed… or worse.

## CHAPTER 2
JADE RIVERS

How much time had passed? I couldn't remember as I pressed a hand into my aching forehead. The room was dark and smelled like laundry detergent but that was it. I blinked to let my eyes adjust to the light but it didn't matter.

"Nalia?" I whispered into the darkness. She should have risen to the surface by now to help with my eyesight. *Nothing.*

"Your wolf won't help you here, girl." The voice startled me and I sat up straight on what I imagined to be the bed.

"Who are you?" My voice trembled into the darkness. Where was I? What happened? How I had gotten here seemed to be a blur.

"I am a prisoner here too," The rough voice

rolled through me and I could feel the power in their wolf even though I couldn't smell them.

Without Nalia, I felt like I couldn't breathe. I felt like I couldn't live. There was a void in my soul that only she could fill. What happened to her? How could I get her back? A sharp pain shot through my temple and I sucked in a quick breath as I doubled over. Chains on the wall clanked together as the shackle on my wrist yanked me back. The back of my head thumped against the wall and a tear leaked from the corner of my eye.

"How long have I been here?" I winced as pain shot through my head again.

"Possibly a week, maybe two." A chain scraped the floor and I realized the man was in the same room as me. Were there others in here with us? "Everything blurs together when you've been drugged and in the dark."

"If you're a prisoner like me then how did you know Nalia was my wolf?" My head was spinning now and all I wanted to do was lie back down to let my consciousness leave me again.

"Nalia is an ancient name, I can feel the power when you say it."

A banging on the door had my back going rigid. I sat up straight and scooted as far away from the sound as I could. The chain scraping the ground from the other side of the room stopped. Bright light blasted through the darkness as a door opened across from me. I sucked a breath between my teeth and closed my eyes. The light still hurt. Moisture flooded my closed eyes and I turned my head down. I couldn't let my captors see me weak. I wouldn't let them see me weak.

"Stop talking in here or you'll be separated." The voice rolled over me in waves and I felt my tongue swell behind my lips. My body wanted to obey but my soul was objecting. It was a new sensation that reminded me of the night Rafe Crimson had forced a change on me. But instead of fighting his Alpha order, I had obeyed. With the order rolling through me from this stranger, I wanted nothing more than to fight it. Pain rolled up my spine but I managed to blink my eyes open and look to the corner of the room. The place where the other stranger was being held.

I sat up straight as I got a good look at him. The man at the door didn't seem to care that I could see as long as we weren't speaking to each other. I relaxed my shoulders and came to a conclusion. I would obey, *for now*. But I would find a way around all of this. The stranger didn't look to be much older than me. His body was thin from being starved and his cheeks were gaunt. His dark brown eyes flashed to mine and his brown skin looked to be coated in a thin sheen of sweat. I held my breath. He had a long beard covering his chin and some of his neck. His dark hair was long past his shoulders in thick waves.

I wouldn't allow them to take me prisoner for much longer. I would fight till my last breath.

Gods save them. I was going to make this place *their* living hell.

The man in the doorway took a step in before he flipped the lights on overhead. I flinched against the brightness again and turned my head down. After the moisture and pain had left my eyes, I lifted my gaze to the gatekeeper of my prison cell. He wore a black ski mask over his face and had a long rifle in his hands. I inhaled hard through my nose.

*Nothing.* His scent was either gone or Nalia's absence was taking a toll on my body. The rest of his clothing was black and thick. I couldn't tell if he was stocky in build or if it was just the baggy clothing.

"Nice to see you've finally decided to join the land of the living," The man's voice was gruff. It sounded like his wolf was ready to come to the surface but his eyes were clear blue before they went a shade darker. "If you keep trying to fight, we will put you down again. There is such a thing as a lethal dose of wolfsbane for your wolf inside you."

What did that mean? I couldn't remember fighting them but that didn't mean I hadn't tried. My hands curled into fists at my sides.

"You would kill off my wolf then?" I sat up straight against the wall. My chains clattered together and echoed around the room.

The man took a step forward and I realized the gun he held wasn't one with bullets, but one with darts instead. "Yes, I will kill your wolf. And do you know what happens to the human side when the wolf is dead?"

My throat dried as I tried to swallow. I didn't want to hear this but I knew I needed to.

"You will die too, except your death will be much longer, much more painful." He twitched his head and it made a loud crack. "And I love to be the one to snuff the life out of wolves."

The door slammed shut behind him but at least he had left the light on. The room we were in looked like a regular bedroom without windows. I was chained to the wall beside a mattress that was on the ground. No box spring or frame to be seen.

The other prisoner didn't even have the luxury I did, but at least his clothes were clean. He leaned against the wall and I noticed the purple spots under his eyes. The walls were white and so were the floors. There was absolutely nothing in the room that I could make into a weapon. I pulled on the shackle around my wrist to test my strength but it was no use, they had somehow made Nalia go away.

My eyes surveyed the walls as the man leaned forward in the corner. "You will not escape here, I hate to break it to you."

"You know nothing about me," I whispered angrily. I wasn't going to go down without a fight. Too many things had happened to me. I wasn't going to continue to be the victim. I was going to save myself. The rest be damned.

"That may be true, but you have no idea where we are. You will get yourself caught and killed trying to play the hero." The man shook his head and the ends of his hair brushed his shoulders.

"Then where are we?" I asked as his eyes flicked to the white door the prison guard had come through.

The man licked his dry, cracked lips. "We are somewhere that nightmares come alive. If you have information they will torture it out of you..." He paused. "There are people here that are held captive in their minds."

My eyes flashed to his. That sounded like Carden. Is this where he had come from?

## CHAPTER 3
TRACEY

I stared down at Jade's phone and braced myself for the call I knew was coming. Jade's parents had been in an area that had spotty service for the last two weeks since Jade's disappearance. It was easy to pretend that Jade was still here.Eventually they would have better service and I couldn't pretend any longer. Jade's cottage that she had gotten in exchange for her job sat in front of me.

The silver key was cold in my other hand. I had been avoiding this for too long. I had told myself every single day that I could do this, but something inside of me shied away.

Everyone else was in an uproar around the pack. No one else would be able to do this. No one but me, even though I wanted to be out there with them, searching for my best friend.

For the fifth time this week, I swiped at the tears streaking down my face. I hadn't been able to stop crying, especially after my body had healed and Jade hadn't come back. It was a nightmare I couldn't wake up from. Every time I closed my eyes I saw Jade being pulled from my wrecked car. No matter how hard I had fought against the seat belt, it had held me into place. My wolf hadn't risen up to help either. This was all my fault.

My fingers trembled as I pushed the key into the lock. The day before I had spent several hours trying to get all the weeds and trees away from the front of the house. Rafe had found me there, collapsed beside the house, covered in sweat. His face was a mask of indifference but I could see it in his eyes. He unclenched his jaw to speak but no words had come out. After a few seconds he sunk down on the ground beside me and we stayed like that until the moon was high in the sky. Oh, how the mighty had fallen.

## CHAPTER 4
JADE RIVERS

My captors hadn't drugged me again, but I could taste the slight undertone of wolfsbane in my food at every meal. They were keeping Nalia contained and it was driving me insane. I felt like myself again, but there was something missing in my soul. A gaping, missing piece right out of the center of my heart. I had learned that the man being held captive with me had been here for years. He had also been turned against his will but he never got the chance to meet his wolf. He wouldn't tell me why. I pushed my tray across the table and looked at him. He had said his name was Lucas but I wondered if it was true. There was a bit of wrongness on the tip of my tongue.

It was the only part of me that reminded me

that Nalia was still with me. We didn't talk while we ate. We just spooned about as much food into our mouths to keep us alive before we sat and watched the others. The others that weren't prisoners, but they were. They walked around like they owned the place but there was something off about it all. They didn't bother to look in our direction or even acknowledge our presence. The guard that had been stationed at our door unshackled us from the table and led us back to the room. They didn't seem to care that we could memorize the long winding hallways. There were no numbers or markers on the doors either. Everything was white and it reminded me of jail, without barred open cells.

When the guard left us shackled again within our room, I turned to Lucas. "Have you tried to get out before?" I whispered. The door was closed and I knew the guard was stationed on the other side, but his hearing was enhanced by his wolf.

Lucas leaned back against the wall. "Yes, and that's why I'm stuck with you."

"What do they have planned for us?"

Lucas raised a shoulder. "My guess is as good as yours is. Right now, all you need to worry about is staying alive and avoiding wolfsbane to keep yourself and your wolf strong."

It was the same mantra every day. Don't drink too much or eat too much. Everything they gave us was laced with wolfsbane. The longer we stayed on it, the harder it would be for our wolves to come back. I laid down on the bed and watched the man on the floor. We had only known each other a few days but I felt bad that he was stuck on the floor.

"Why don't you have a bed?"

His brown eyes flicked up to mine and a shadow passed over his face. "I tried to free you."

I sat up. "Why would you do such a thing?"

He shrugged up a shoulder then sunk down to the floor. "Why not? You don't deserve to be here."

"And you do?"

He pressed his lips together and turned away from me. So much for getting to know him better.

## CHAPTER 5
TRACEY

The call never came. I waited and waited for Jade's parents to ring her but they never did. The service must have cut out where they were. I ran my finger over the scar on my forearm and sighed. I didn't have a single scar on my body. But this one was there to remind me of the night I had failed our entire pack. If something happened to Jade, then our Alpha was doomed. This had probably been the plan from the start with the rogues... or whoever they were and we had played right into their hands.

We should have told Jade the truth from the very beginning.

My hands burned from the chemicals I scrubbed into the tiles on the bathroom floor of

Jade's cottage. I released the rag with a ragged sigh and sat back on the balls of my feet in a crouch. I had been at this for hours now, hoping to keep my mind off of everything that had happened. I was also trying to keep my mind off of the things that could be happening. I wasn't doing a very good job of it. My eyes burned and internally I blamed it on the cleaner I had been using. I tossed the rag into the sink and pushed up to my full height. The kitchen was clean, not spotless, but clean enough. The laundry room no longer had a rat problem and was ready for a washer and dryer. The living room's carpet was pulled up and the wood floor that had been hidden underneath needed a good shine job.

I whirled as someone knocked on the front door. Thankfully the mirror was still covered in a thick grime and I didn't have to see myself as I walked by. When I yanked the door open it dispelled a wave of dust. No matter what I did, I couldn't seem to get rid of all the dirt in the air. It would take me weeks to get this place in tip-top condition.

My mom waited on the other side of the door. Her white hair was pulled up away from her face in her typical fashion. She wore loose jeans and a sweater. She didn't look a day over thirty but there was a weariness to her eyes today.

I took a step back. "What's up?"

She held up a soda and a bag full of food. My stomach growled in response as my wolf purred in my head. I took the bag from her hands and moved out of the doorway for her to come inside. "I figured you were hungry. You've been in here for a while."

I rolled my eyes. "It hasn't been that long."

My mom gave me a stern look. "It's been twelve hours."

The bag threatened to spill from my fingers. "What?"

"It's dinner time," She threw me a concerned look. "Do you need to talk?"

Did I? Probably. Was I going to? No.

I shrugged my shoulders and sunk down onto the tile in the kitchen. It was the cleanest part of the tiny house. It was the first place I had started on. It smelled like lemons now.

"You don't need to hide it all from me. Let me be the one to take the burden from your shoulders."

I scoffed. "And how are you going to do that?"

She sighed and slid down to the floor. She stretched her legs out and leaned against the cabinets across from me. "Let me help you."

I ruffled through the bag so I didn't have to look

at her. She had brought me a rare steak and mashed potatoes. I immediately dug in instead of acknowledging what she said. My parents were very different people. Getting emotional and having a breakdown hadn't been allowed. At least, not when it came to my older brother. I scrunched my nose up to keep the tears from coming again. I could only look so weak around my parents. My father was the opposite of my mother in every way. My mom tried to be the healing salve to his abrasiveness.

"You can't do this all on your own, this isn't even your home to fix."

The potatoes tasted like ash on my tongue as my eyes rose to meet hers. I swallowed quickly. "There are two bedrooms."

Her face softened at that. "Honey,"

I shook my head sharply before I ate some more of the food that tasted like nothing. My stomach was happy but my heart was not.

"This is her home, and…" She paused and her face fell. "What if she doesn't come back?"

I shrugged one of my shoulders up. "None of this matters then. Not one bit of it."

"The pack will go on. There is a Beta for a reason." Her husband, my father. But I couldn't acknowledge that either. It was all too much. I finished the food quickly, not tasting a thing.

Jade had to come back. She had parents that had fought so long to have her. She had me that finally felt like I belonged. She had the guys that loved her and just wanted to see her smile. And then she had Rafe, the insufferable bastard. The insufferable bastard that didn't know how to do anything right but he was good, somewhere deep down. I knew he was good. I had known it the first time I shifted.

It had been in the middle of the grocery store. He was a few years older than me. I didn't leave his side. I wanted to go everywhere with the Alpha's son. So I tailed him to the grocery store and I hadn't even shifted yet. Everyone said I was a late bloomer. Turns out my wolf just liked a little bit of exhibition. He had wrapped his coat around me and carried me out of the store. Joked that his puppy had followed him. For years that had been my nickname. *Puppy.* Until we grew up and everyone stopped whispering that we were destined to be mates. There was a part of me that had always wondered if the mate bond was just a little late like my shift had been. But then it happened with someone else and I didn't know how to process it. I didn't even think he had realized before he was shipped off to Pack Law to become a Guardian and I was left behind.

I pressed my palms into my eyes as my nose burned and my eyes watered. I was always left behind. My mom leaned over and wrapped her arms around me as the tears slipped free again. It didn't matter if there was a Beta. It didn't matter if things didn't work out because how was I going to survive if the others didn't? My best friends...

**CHAPTER 6**
JADE

The days came and went. I didn't know how long I had been in here and I started to not care. I didn't care as I was carted into the co-ed bathroom or as I was forced to strip down before my guard and Lucas. I became a shell of the human I had once been in a short course of time. They were trying to break me and it was working.

The cold water pelted my back and I no longer felt it. I could no longer feel anything but every day Lucas's eyes would stare into mine like he could will my wolf back. Like he could bring me back from the emotions I had drowned in.

A stiff towel was shoved into my arms as the water shut off. I didn't even care if the soap was washed from me all the way. At one point I had cared, I had scrubbed and scrubbed until my skin was red. But those days had come and gone faster than I wanted to admit. The fight in me was dying out. I could feel Lucas's eyes on me as I dried off with what felt like sandpaper. I didn't dare look at him. The guard didn't like how much we talked. I didn't want to know what would happen if he thought there was something happening between us. Which there wasn't but it didn't matter. He was watching me now and it would be too much. So I ignored him.

My shoulders slumped forward as the towel was ripped from my fingers, a shift dress was thrown at me. It was different from the scrubs I had been forced to wear. The rough dress fell above my knees in an indecent manner for the human world. But around here, did it matter? I had seen a manner of all different kinds of clothing on the prisoners that didn't look like prisoners. I had even seen some wear fishnets for clothing, their nakedness on display for the rest of the prison to see. Not one person had blinked an eye. I had seen the horror on Lucas's face but I didn't question him. He had said he had been forced into this life.

Our bare feet dragged on the concrete floors as we walked back to the room. But something felt different. I couldn't pinpoint it so I looked up for the first time in a week and met Lucas's stare. His jaw was clenched and his eyes were ablaze with fight. The guard was ignoring us both but there was a slight twitch under his left eye.

Our door opened up and Lucas was shoved into the room as the guard shackled me to himself. Lucas turned and let out a snarl before he came barreling at us. The guard slammed the door in his face. The doorframe glowed blue as Lucas pounded on it.

"Looks like the little witch has taken a liking to you." The guard snickered and my back went straight at the new information. "Oh, he didn't tell you? Yes, witches can be turned but its a very painful process. He suffered for weeks before he finally gave himself up to the wolf. You should have seen him fight."

Nausea rolled through me as he jerked me down the hall, away from Lucas. Were they finally separating us? "Where are you taking me?"

"The big boss is ready to see you now." And that was all he said as he dragged me down the hallway on weak legs. I tried to keep up but his strides were too long and my legs were too weak from not eating much each day. Just enough to keep myself alive but not enough to bring in too much wolfsbane. I could smell it now when I went to eat. I knew which foods were laced stronger. Like the meat. The meat was filled with it but other things like potatoes or mac and cheese didn't have nearly as much. My body hated the sides and needed the protein desperately but I couldn't allow myself to be any weaker. I wanted to escape but I didn't know if I had it in me.

"Keep your head down or he will rip your throat out." The guard whispered to me. I blinked and looked up at him. His eyes were dark blue again, instead of the piercing white blue they normally were. He led me to a set of massive double doors. They slid open to reveal massive steps that led to another set of double doors. The click of the lock seemed to echo off of the walls as he unlocked the handcuffs around my wrist. The need to rub my raw wrists was overwhelming. I kept my arms at my sides as he walked me to the top of the stairs. My legs protested with each climb and by the top of them, I was winded. I sucked in big gulps of air before the doors in front of us were shoved open.

There in the middle of the room was a man. He was all alone with a woman kneeling at his feet. She had a silver collar around her throat. I almost missed it with the way her orange hair fell around her shoulders. She was dressed in a bodysuit that fit from right below her neck and went down her legs before it disappeared inside a pair of black lace boots. The man cocked his head and my attention was brought to him. I couldn't feel his power, but I could see it in his eyes. They were depthless and the green in them seemed to go on for an eternity. They were eyes that would bewitch you. I tried to pull my gaze away to observe his other features. He wore a similar outfit to the woman on the floor and his black hair was long enough to brush the top buttons on his own dark bodysuit.

"Hello there," his voice purred around me like he was beside me and not several feet away. "It is so nice to finally meet you."

I shivered against the feeling of his presence beside me, even though he was so far away. His chin lifted a notch as his eyes roved over my body. "And what is your name?"

I could feel the defiance rising up within me. I gritted my teeth. "You already know my name, don't pretend otherwise." The fight that had seemed to disappear from me in the last week was back with a vengeance.

His lips lifted in a mock smile and I noted his long canines. "Yes, Jade Rivers, I know everything there is to know about you. I know where you go to school. All the classes you take. The vacations your parents frequent."

My blood went cold at that admonition. I tried to keep the look off of my face but I knew he could feel the shift in me.

"Your parents aren't my concern, at least not yet. If I had prepared my men accordingly I would have used them to my advantage and kept them from leaving." He shrugged like it didn't matter one bit.

"What do you want from me?" Anything to keep the topic off of my parents. Would they be protected by the pack even with me gone now? Would Rafe protect them? If not him, would Tracey. As werewolves, we accepted the responsibility of the humans that lived around us. We pledged ourselves as their guardians.

"There are many things I want from you but for now, I want to know about your mate bond."

All I could do was frown. "Mate bond?"

His lips curled up into an actual smile. "You

don't know then. That explains the lack of claim marks, but it doesn't explain your wolf lurking below your skin."

Something inside of me rose up. Something wanted to tell him about the dreaded night when everything had changed but I knew better. The guard beside me brushed me with his hand and clarity came back to me. I wouldn't tell this man a thing about me or my past. If he wanted to know so badly, he could find it out on his own.

He cocked his head and the smile slipped from his face. "You aren't as talkative as I like." His eyes snapped to the guard beside me. "Is she eating enough?"

The guard bowed his head before he spoke. "Yes, she is eating most of her meals."

I blinked. It was all I could do to not give his lie away. He knew I wasn't eating all of my meals.

The man in front of us frowned. His dark brows pulled together. "Is the wolfsbane not strong enough? She should have bent to my will."

"Is that how you do it then? You drug us all and expect us to be complacent." A red tinge washed through his bronzed face as I spoke. "You will never have what you seek. Your power doesn't come from within, it comes from a drug. You will never have anything. You are weak." I didn't know where the words came from because they certainly weren't my own. For a moment I felt hope. I knew without a shadow of a doubt that somehow Nalia had broken through.

## CHAPTER 7
RAFE

*A member of our pack has been kidnapped.* No matter how many times I rehearsed in the mirror, I couldn't get it right. I rolled my shoulders and stared at my reflection. Technically, it wasn't a lie but it still smelled like it in the air. I had to get it right or we would never get aid from the other packs. We wouldn't get aid from Pack Law.

Why hadn't I told her? I pressed my palms into the counter and bowed my head. All of this was my fault because I didn't want to sway her feelings. I hadn't wanted to make this about fate, but about her. But now that she was gone, the rest of the pack was going to have to know what happened. Why it needed to happen. I hadn't wanted to share in case it got back to Jade. All I wanted was for her to feel comfortable. Forcing this lifestyle on her, forcing her wolf on her had been more than I wanted to do. But it was something I had to do. I wanted her to understand that before all of this came out. I wanted her to know that I wasn't all villain in her story. I wanted her to know that things could have been different if we had time, but unfortunately, that was stolen from the both of us. We could have done things normal, but life was never that way.

The door opened behind me and Knox came into view. His auburn hair was tied up in a loose ponytail and his face was grim. I didn't look forward to the updates. The updates that hadn't changed.

"Still nothing. I called Archer to come back home." Knox didn't sound like it was something he wanted to do but the trail had run cold. I already knew it though. I had run and run through the woods and all the roads until there was nothing left. I had searched high and low for something, anything, but came up with nothing. I had followed her scent until it ran dry and the only other options were going into other packs. They had passed through other territories and that was why I needed help. As much as I wanted to do it on my own, I knew I couldn't.

"I have called a pack meeting," My voice didn't sound like my own and I wondered when it would permanently stay this way. The growly undertone had appeared the night Jade had been kidnapped and hadn't disappeared since. My wolf was close to the surface and anything could set him off at this point.

**CHAPTER 8**
JADE

The room I was returned to wasn't the one I had been in before. When we stopped at the black door I looked at the guard beside me. Could I trust him? Did I acknowledge the lie that he had spoken in my favor? There was a slight twitch to his head and it took me a minute to realize he was shaking it. He was telling me to be quiet.

"Where is Lucas? Why am I being put here?" I was going to be difficult. I could already feel it in my bones.

"The commander wants to ask you a few questions." Disgust coated his whispered words. "You aren't to ask any more questions."

He unshackled me and threw me into the darkened room. My legs buckled beneath me as I scrambled across the floor. The room was no bigger than a supply closet and it was completely empty. There was a dim light on the ceiling but that was it. The floors were concrete. It took a few minutes before the door opened again and the man that had been called the big boss entered. The woman that had kneeled at his feet wasn't with him. The metal gleamed on the knife in his hand. I swallowed as I took a step away from him. All he did was lean against the door as he looked me over again.

"Do you know why you're here?" His voice was soft. Deceiving.

I shook my head. I didn't trust my voice. After Nalia had taken over my speech, I had been cast from the room. He had nothing else to say to me and I knew that a storm would be coming. The storm was here now.

"Do you know who your mate is?" Through some fogginess in my brain, I recalled something. There was that feeling inside of me at the word like I knew. Like someone had told me but I couldn't remember.

I shook my head.

"What is your rank within the pack?"

I blinked at him. His voice was void of all emotion as he watched me. I grasped my hands in front of me and wondered why I hadn't been chained down. Was this man that confident or was I that weak? I shrugged my shoulders.

He narrowed his green eyes and leaned forward. The slight movement made me flinch. What were his plans for me? Was the knife simply for self-defense or something more? "I would like to get to know you better, Jade Rivers. I would like to know who you are behind the mask you wear currently. I want to know your hopes and your dreams. I would like to think that we could be more to each other. We could help each other. We could be *friends.*"

"How would we do that?" My voice trembled and I hated myself for it.

"I hear that you have wanted revenge against Rafe Crimson." There it was. That was why I was here. Was this Pack Law? Had they heard I wanted to hurt an Alpha? An Alpha that was worth more than my life was?

His lips twitched before they transformed into a smile and my blood ran cold. The smile was radiant but calculating. Terrifying. "I have wanted revenge against Rafe Crimson for a long time."

I nodded my head and eased forward like I could participate in what he was offering but I didn't trust him. This wasn't Pack Law. They wouldn't want revenge against the man that had turned me against my will, would they? Pack Law wouldn't hold hundreds of wolves prisoner in their own bodies, right? He reached forward and ran a finger down my bare arm.

"Yes," he breathed. "I do believe we can come to a partnership between us. Possibly even more down the road."

I swallowed hard and hoped that all it did was solidify how afraid I was. I didn't want him to know that I was nervous. I knew he could scent my emotions in the air.

I paused. Or could he? I hadn't seen any proof that he was an actual wolf himself. His eyes didn't glow yellow and he seemed rather normal. But didn't all the true monsters?

"I heard down the grapevine that you love a bad boy?" The blade replaced his fingers and I shivered against the cool touch of the knife. "What if I'm bad?"

I couldn't have fought the next shiver even if I wanted to. His words were like a balm to the fear inside of me. I pressed my lips together before I cocked my head at him.

*Then we will become worse.* Nalia's whisper in my mind was weak but full of determination. My eyes met his and I smiled. A partnership wouldn't be such a bad thing.

## CHAPTER 9
TRACEY

The house was spotless, but it was missing life. It was missing Jade's life and light. It was missing everything that made her *her*. I had done my best to design it in the aesthetic that I knew she would love. I painted until my head hurt and my fingers were calloused from holding a paintbrush. My arms trembled and my legs felt weak as I went through all the motions. I broke down as I painted, as I pulled flooring up and laid it down. I cried as I walked down the aisles of the home improvement store looking for any item that screamed *Jade*.

All the furniture I bought left me hollow. Every store ripped me up more inside. I thought it would bring me closer to her, but at the end of it, all it did was make me feel empty. I couldn't bring myself to sit on the couch or admire my handiwork.

Someone had knocked on the door hours ago, but I had ignored it as I sat in the living room and died inside some more. My mom didn't come back to visit but she had offered on countless occasions to go to the store with me. She had offered to scour the internet for me. She had offered and offered and *offered* but all I said was no. I couldn't do it with anyone else because the one person I needed to do all of it with wasn't here and didn't have a choice. How could I bring someone else in on this project?

Instead of a knock, there was a pounding on the door this time. I didn't look up from the wood floor beneath me. "I swear on everything good that if you don't open this door, I will burn this cottage down."

Stupid Knox and his infuriating pestering. He hadn't spoken much to me since he had returned. Even on the way home from the airport, he had been silent. All he could provide were broody looks and long glances. Neither of which I wanted. I ignored him. He wouldn't burn down Jade's cottage because if he did that he would bring down Rafe's wrath upon him and no one wanted that. Rafe's wolf hadn't been persuaded to back down in weeks. He was close to the edge and everyone knew it. It was another reason I had stayed holed up in here. There was no point in agitating his wolf anymore. The full moon was tomorrow and I wondered how he was going to fare.

"Open up, Tracey." This time it was Rafe. I sat up straight and jumped to open the door. He actually sounded like himself, if not slightly tired, which was to be expected.

Knox and Rafe stood side by side in the doorway. In between them was a massive box. For the first time, in a long time, I felt good. The sight of the box between them and what was in it had me excited. Excited because I knew it was exactly what Jade wanted. I had kept myself from snooping on her phone but I did look in her online shopping cart. The first item in there was a massive gold-plated canopy bed. The one that was now in pieces between the two men in front of me. I bit my bottom lip before I grinned.

I pressed the tips of my fingers to my chin before I motioned them to come inside. There was a slight thud behind me and the clanging of metal hitting each other. I turned on my heel ready to light into them when I realized they had dropped the box because of the surprise they were feeling. Rafe's jaw was slack staring at all the work I had done and Knox was staring at me with bright eyes. His red hair was down today and around his shoulders. I looked away before I could get a sniff of his emotions. I had tried my hardest not to scent the people around me lately. I couldn't handle the bone-crushing despair they all felt. I knew all too well what it was like and I didn't need a reminder that others were feeling it too. Not for Jade's benefit but for mine. They were sad for me, not the newcomer they didn't know. I had been a part of this pack my entire life. They felt pity for me and I couldn't stand it.

But I could see it in Knox's eyes, he didn't feel pity. He felt awe.

Rafe was the first to speak. "You did all of this?"

I nodded, not trusting my voice or my emotions one bit.

"All alone?" Rafe asked again.

Knox snorted. "There have been plenty of offers to help."

My eyes snapped to his. "You spoke to my mother?"

He jutted his chin up in defiance. "She spoke to me. She wanted to see if I could get through to you."

My shoulders tensed. Nope. I wasn't going there. "You can bring the box down the hall. This way, please."

The sounds of them lifting and carrying the box followed me to the hallway that held two bedrooms and a bathroom. Jade's bedroom didn't have a bathroom but I had already had plans drawn up for one to be added on. It wouldn't cost very much and I knew Jade would want her privacy. At her home with her parents, I could see the love she had for her own space.

I tucked my hands into my pockets as I nudged her door open with the toe of my boot. The room still smelled like wet paint and the burger I had devoured in the corner at lunch. I had painted her bedroom white and had installed dark hardwood floors. The wall that the bed would go on was black and a gold circular mirror hung from the center of it. Now with the bed about to go there, I knew it would go better over the black dresser that would sit on the opposite wall. I was simply waiting for it to be delivered too. It had also been in Jade's online cart. I hadn't wanted to decorate her room or buy anything until I knew it was what she would want. Thankfully, she had her entire bedroom furniture picked out already and waiting to be purchased. It was the least I could do. Especially since all of this was my fault. I had been the idiot that night. I hadn't been careful enough. I hung my head as the men hefted the massive box into the room and sat it in the middle of the floor. Knox wouldn't look at me and I didn't care. I was done caring what anyone else thought.

The tip of my finger extended into a sharp claw and I cut down the middle of the box. Clanking echoed around the empty room as the pieces of the bed rolled out onto the dark floor.

"Is she going to like these things?" Rafe looked pained as he took it all in. I couldn't blame him, it made me feel the same. *Guilty*.

I nodded my head. I didn't need to explain myself. I knew Jade far better than any of them did. Rafe had made sure of that. He had handpicked all of my classes to be with hers. He hadn't known if she lived on campus or not so he had organized for me to live there, just in case. It added to my story. He had someone follow her at the grocery store to figure out the foods she liked. I knew her better than everyone because it had been my mission to do so. But I also knew her better than anyone because even through all of this, she had still called me. She had still texted me when she knew things weren't as they seemed. She had trusted me even though I wasn't to be trusted at all. She had given me a chance to be her friend.

All of my motives had been sour from the start but she had come to trust me and I wouldn't ever do another thing to put that in jeopardy again. Her friendship had become such a bright spot in my life. In my boring life. I loved Rafe. He had been like a brother to me after I had realized we would never be mates. I had followed him and the Guardians around like they were my older brothers, before they swore their lives to Rafe's. They were my family but Jade had always been a choice I was glad I made. She was the one thing that I had chosen for a good reason, rather than a selfish one.

The friendships and relationships within the pack had a certain order. It was how it was done. There was no changing it. There were social circles and friendships I was never allowed in simply because of my dominance as a female. *The abomination of the dominance.* I had listened to the whispers around the pack growing up. I knew that I wasn't supposed to have so much fire and determination in my wolf. That it was because my brother was a witch and somehow, I had taken his wolf because the wolf didn't choose him. My mother told me not to listen, but my little wolf ears had picked every word up. I had devoured the negative energy and tried my hardest to harness it into something good. Something better than them. My mother called them the busybodies. They had nothing better to do with their time but be jealous of a tiny child.

I shook my head. Those were thoughts for another time. I needed to numb myself. I needed to get lost in the task and let my mind go.

Knox's words hit me like a physical blow. "How do you know she would even want you to do this for her? What if all of this will just make her angry? This is her home, not yours."

I ground my teeth together as I stood up from my numbing task. The numbing wouldn't take effect until they went away. I cracked my neck as I came face to face with the bastard. His nostrils flared as I took a step toward him. "What if she never comes back? Then none of this matters. Leave me be and let me handle my grief in the only way I know how. Why don't you do what you do best? Go find a whore house, get sloppy, then find my friend. Isn't that the only thing you are good for anyway? Being a *soldier*."

I spat the last word like a curse. I knew I was being nasty. I knew the things I said hurt and I liked it. It was the only thing that didn't make me feel terrible inside.

## CHAPTER 10
JADE

"I want to know your name," I finally said after a few minutes. We had stood there, locked in each other's gaze without saying a word.

He shrugged as he placed the knife on the floor. A peace offering. "I will answer your questions but only if you answer mine."

I cocked an eyebrow. "A question for a question then."

He ran his tongue over his teeth. "This feels like we are fifteen and playing twenty-one questions."

I chose to ignore the comment. There was no need for flirty banter. I was gonna go along with his plan but I wasn't going to do so at the expense of myself. Of my body. There were other ways I could win.

He leaned against the wall again and watched me with heavy eyes. "Here, they simply call me the boss but I once had a name, a long time ago."

I narrowed my eyes at him. It wasn't an answer. I pressed my lips together. "Fine," He looked up at the ceiling and his eyes crinkled in the corners in what I imagined was amusement. "Damian."

That wasn't so bad. He looked like a Damian. "Am I allowed to call you that?"

He smirked. "It's my turn to ask a question."

I nodded my head. It was going to be like that.

"Why didn't you join the Crimson Pack?"

That was a complex question with a complex answer. "I don't like Rafe Crimson."

He took a step toward me. "I know that much. But *why?*"

"He turned me against my will." It wasn't the only reason but I didn't have to give him all of that. He cocked an eyebrow and nodded his head. He knew the answer already but was testing me.

"What did Rafe do to you?"

Damian flashed his teeth. "He was born."

I rolled my eyes. "How vague."

"He has been my rival for a very long time. Everything he did was thrown in my face. I could never live up to the wolf he is. I was never enough."

I wanted more, I scented a story in the air but I knew I couldn't pry. There was only so much this man would give. I would have to be careful.

He cracked his neck as he thought of his question. Maybe he was just hesitating for my benefit. He probably had all his questions planned out in his head. "Are you going to tell your parents what you are?"

The question stunned me. I blinked abruptly. "Probably not."

He nodded his head like he expected that. "You'll be relieved to know that we haven't bothered them since that night. Since the night the ball was thrown through the window."

I narrowed my eyes at him. "Why did you do that?"

"I wanted to get you away from them, away from the pack. Rafe was becoming a problem for my people."

I rolled my shoulders. Pain from standing in the same position was starting to get to me. I had no idea how long I would be standing there but I wished desperately for a chair. My body was too weak to keep going like this.

"Your people?"

He wagged his finger at me. "It's my turn to ask

a question." He ran his fingers down his jaw. "Where do you think your parents think you are now?"

I had dreaded it. I had dreaded the thought of how they were coping with my disappearance. I had been physically ill thinking about them and what they were going through. "Dead."

He smiled and my blood ran cold. "They know you're safe."

He was baiting me to use up all my questions on things that didn't matter to him, but on things that only mattered to me. "What did you do?"

Elongated canines poked his bottom lip as he continued to look me over. "The great thing about having witches in my employ is that they can manipulate anything. Your body, your voice, even reality."

My legs ached. I sunk to the floor and bowed my head. What had he done? Had he smoothed everything over? Had he made everything worse? How was I going to recover anything when I got out of here?

## CHAPTER 11
TRACEY

I took a steadying breath as I turned down the street Jade's home was on. I was too much of a chicken to call her parents. How was I going to explain all of these weeks gone? How was I going to explain anything to them? I had zero answers and just as much heartache as I was allowing myself to feel. I didn't know how to prepare myself for when they got home and I would have to break the news to them in person. I ran one of my sweaty hands down my leg and then slammed on my brakes.

I was only a few houses down from her's, but I could see clear as day that the Rivers were home. I was about to backtrack when Jade's mom lifted her head from the mailbox and waved to me. She didn't look worried. Her eyes were bright and her skin looked good, a healthy tan from probably being in the sun a lot in the east. I couldn't tuck tail and run now.

Somehow I pulled into their driveway and got out of the car. Somehow I walked up to the door where Mrs. Rivers was waiting for me. Her lips formed a genuine smile but there was some sadness in her eyes.

"Hi, Mrs. Rivers," I started before I paused then swallowed hard. "How have you been?"

She placed a hand on her hip. "I should be asking you that, you look terrible. Have you even been eating?"

I shrugged my shoulders. "Not really."

She sighed. Her hair was pulled into a ponytail on the top of her head and she didn't look a day over thirty, even with her silver hair. "Jade told me that the fight was bad between the two of you but I had no idea it was this bad."

"Fight?" My voice shook. What was going on? Was Jade back? "Is Jade here?"

Mrs. Rivers ran her hand down the length of my arm as she led me inside. Mr. Rivers was nowhere to be found. I wondered if he was actually in the office, working. I knew he did some sort of accounting, it was where Jade got her love for numbers.

"She must not have told you because of everything that happened." Mrs. Rivers' words felt like physical blows. Jade's phone in my back pocket felt like a weight. "She is still on a trip with her work, you know she got a job with the Crimson's, right?"

I nodded my head slowly. I didn't know where we were going with this but I couldn't turn away now. My chest didn't feel so tight for the first time in weeks. Maybe this would get us closer to finding answers. Maybe she escaped and she had run away to get out of all the madness that came with our kind. All sorts of speculations swirled around in my head.

Mrs. Rivers held her phone up and showed off a grinning Jade in front of the Grand Canyon. She had a loose sweater on and baggy jeans. Her hair was pulled into two tight braids on either side of her head. She held her thumb up and I knew that it wasn't her. I smiled but I felt my stomach drop. Whoever had her was doing a good job of keeping her disappearance from the press.

"Have you spoken to her on the phone?" My voice sounded faraway to my own ears.

Mrs. Rivers nodded. "Yes, she calls me more

than ever. She sounds so happy and full of life. If we had known that giving her independence would help her flourish then we would have encouraged it a long time ago."

They were talking on the phone?

"She told you about our fight? What did she say?"

Mrs. Rivers's face fell. "She said that she didn't have any intention of speaking to you in a while. That lots of hurtful things were said because of something that happened at a party a while back?"

I twisted my hands in front of me. "Yeah, I thought we had gotten over that. I didn't realize she was still so upset."

I had to do anything to find out more information, even if it meant continuing the lie. There was powerful magic involved, I had no doubt.

"I always liked the friendship she had with you. Her whole life she was alone. She had friends but never let anyone very close. It always worried me and honestly, I felt like it was my fault. As we went through infertility before we had her, I stopped trying to have friends. The pain was too unbearable to be around others that had no problems getting pregnant. It was always easier to friend people in other countries that we didn't have to see often."

I nodded my head. Some of this I had already known.

She sighed. "She said she didn't want to speak to you... but I feel like you should call her. She always cared for you and I don't want her to lose the only real friend she has."

She held out her phone to me so I could take down the number into mine. I didn't miss the other pics of her smiling in similar baggy clothes on the screen of the texts. "Can you not tell her that I have this? I feel like I need to work up the nerve to speak to her. I need to think of what I want to say to her. I miss her so much."

Mrs. Rivers grabbed my hand in hers before she pulled me in for a hug. "She loves you, I think she's just a little lost at the moment."

She didn't know how right she was.

## CHAPTER 12
RAFE

The phone in my hands felt like a bomb about to go off. I ran my fingers through my hair again before I threw the phone through the wall. I could barely contain the rage flowing through my limbs. Jinx, one of the lower-ranking wolves in the pack, had been able to trace the phone number that Tracey had gotten from Jade's mother. None of it was good. The phone number was linked to one of the witch covens on the other side of the Racer Pack. We couldn't go through their territory without permission but we had no idea if they were working together either.

When my father had been Alpha things had been strained between our two packs for hundreds of years. I had no reason to patch things up. I had no reason to dig up old memories of my old man before he got sick. I also didn't have much reason to bring it up to my mom… until now.

She was watching me across the table, with my brother. My brother ignored my gaze as he shoveled food into his mouth. My mother, however, had her eyes set on me. Neither of us had touched our food. I leaned back in my chair and crossed my arms over my chest. The phone was now discarded on the table.

"Tell me about the Racer Pack," All the commotion at the table skidded to a halt. My mother's eyebrow quirked slightly as she rose from the table and walked down the hall. I knew where she was headed before I stood from my chair. I ground my teeth together as I followed behind her.

The smell of Jade was faint now, but it was enough to make me flinch as I pushed the office door closed behind me. She had bought a little succulent for her desk and had brought a water bottle from home. There was a pen set neatly next to the monitor. Those were the only traces of her here.

I rubbed the center of my chest with my fist as I tried to process all the emotions flooding me.

"Your uncle is the Alpha of the Racer Pack,"

My head snapped up at the words. My mom leaned back in the office chair and closed her eyes. "He left this pack for a number of reasons but the first one was when your father chose a wife."

I leaned against the wall and took a deep breath. This was a story that I wasn't ready to hear, but also, a story that my mother needed to tell. I could see it on her face, how much pain it was causing her to keep it all in. To keep it all together. Her shoulders relaxed an inch.

"She was a witch," I watched as my mom's throat bobbed and the air filled with her nervous scent. "There was already enough turmoil with the witch covens at the time. Your father thought marrying one would be a good thing. Axel, Tracey's dad, had married a half-witch. He had mated with her. What was the big deal?"

I ran my hand down my face and she continued.

"He thought the mate bond would just snap into place eventually, but there were complications and eventually she died." Complications? I narrowed my eyes. What were the complications? How long ago was this? I pressed my lips together even though all of my thoughts and questions fought to come out. "That was at least a hundred years ago. There was much that happened after that but apparently, your uncle was in love with her. When she died, he was devastated. He told your father he was never allowed to come through the pack again. That he would never be welcomed back or forgiven. The covens eventually forgave your father because it wasn't his fault. Complications with pregnancy happened all the time, especially when mixing supernatural races. Your Uncle Jared never got over it, unfortunately. We haven't seen or heard from the Racer Pack since."

I exhaled through my nose and shook my head. Was he involved in this? Was he working with the witches and the rogues?

## CHAPTER 13
JADE

It had been two days since Damian and I had exchanged questions and answers. Two days since I had seen Lucas, the man from my cell. Two days since I had been placed in a regular bedroom without my shackles. The guard was the same, the one I knew would help me escape, but I needed to find the opportunity to do so. My wrists were still raw from the cuffs that had been around them. The werewolf healing I was supposed to have was gone still, thanks to the wolfsbane in my food.

I was given proper clothing and my bed smelled clean but I didn't feel better. I didn't feel even remotely okay. Lucas was somewhere getting the same crappy treatment and I couldn't stand for that to continue.

For the first time since I had been deposited into this room, I got the guts to explore it. It took two days for me to be comfortable enough to do so. I had a light switch inside, rather than on the other side of the door. There were zero chains on or around the bed. One of the three doors in the room led to my guard, another to an empty closet, and then the last was a bathroom. An actual bathroom that I didn't have to share with anyone else. A bathroom that I could use whenever I wanted. It wasn't much, but it was a luxury I never knew I would miss.

I knocked on the first door and the guard opened it. He was still wearing a ski mask but I knew immediately he was the same man from the first day. I straightened my shoulders. "I want to see Lucas."

His voice was gruff as his eyes changed to a bright yellow. "That isn't something I can permit."

"Then talk to someone that can." I folded my arms over my chest.

He sighed. "Is this your *one* request?"

I raised my eyebrows. "I get one request?"

"One that is reasonable, yes. For your cooperation."

I nodded my head. He was someone I hoped

would be a friend. I didn't know much about him but I knew he didn't deserve to be here anymore than I did.

He grabbed the door handle. "Fine, but you're the one who asked for this. Remember that." The door closed without another word.

My one request was granted later that day while I was eating my dinner in silence. I had avoided the meat but I had a feeling, they knew what I was up to. The mashed potatoes tasted bitter and the salad had a weird glaze on the leaves. The meat seemed to be the most normal thing. The door slammed open while I was lifting the fork to my lips. It bounced off of the wall and in walked my guard, with Lucas in tow. The guard shook his head and slammed the door behind him.

Lucas didn't look happy to see me. "What did you do?"

I pushed my tray to him. He ignored it.

"What did you do, Jade?" he repeated the question.

"I had one request and I used it to get you here. Now I am not so lonely and now you don't have to be in such awful conditions."

His brows pulled together. "You're pretty stupid, has anyone told you that before?"

I frowned. "That isn't very nice."

He snorted. "Do you know what isn't very nice? They are using you. They want you to get close to someone," he pointed at himself. "So they can use that person against you."

My stomach dropped and I was thankful I had stopped eating. I didn't feel so good now. His shoulders dropped as he caught the look on my face.

"I couldn't figure out why they had paired us together until now. There are plenty of prisoners here that fight their wolves, I am nothing special." He sat down on the floor beside me before he pulled the tray of food to himself.

"You're fighting your wolf?"

He shrugged a shoulder up. "I don't see why it matters. They did this to me. I have no choice but me and my wolf don't exactly have the opportunity not to fight. All this wolfsbane is killing me."

"I don't plan on staying here that long." I shrugged as I watched him eat. I had missed having his company even if it didn't amount to much. He was broody and quiet. I didn't know much about him at all.

"What did you do, sell your soul to the devil?"

I quirked an eyebrow. "Damian?"

"He might as well be the devil himself, Jade. You have no idea what you have done. Do you at least know why you're here?"

I wanted to answer his questions. It was so nice to be able to talk to someone besides the villain, but I knew better. I couldn't trust Lucas just yet, even if I wanted to. Even if I was lonely. I still didn't know him, but I didn't want to be alone.

"Why are you here?" He had to know that.

He swallowed a mouthful of water before he looked at me. His eyes were brown and they held so much sadness. He reminded me of an abandoned puppy. But I knew looks could be deceiving. I had let myself get wrapped up with the wrong man one too many times. I couldn't let puppy dog eyes get me in trouble this time.

His eyes met mine and he smiled. It was a smile that could steal someone's breath away. It was completely unexpected. "I see that I haven't given you much to trust, have I?"

I shook my head once.

"I was in the wrong place at the wrong time. I was traveling between covens, learning about my people when Damian found me. At first," he paused and looked away from me. His hair moved away from his neck and I caught a glimpse of darker skin, healed skin. Then it was gone. "I thought what he was offering was a new world, a new world where Pack Law didn't exist and wolves didn't have to worry about rank or the ridicule that came from it. But then I saw his true agenda and I tried to run." He took a deep breath. "I tried to run, to get to my family, I needed to notify them of this. But it was too late. Damian had used venom to change me. He forced a wolf on me and I tried to take my life after the full moon."

That explained the darkened skin on his neck. I pinched my lips together and looked at my clasped hands in my lap. "I'm so sorry."

The fork clanked on the plate. "Do not apologize unless you plan on working for him."

"I plan on doing no such thing. He didn't tell me his agenda either. He just wants my help with revenge, he said."

Lucas leaned back on his hands. "He wants so much more than revenge, Jade."

## CHAPTER 14
TRACEY

The cottage was finished. I turned the key in the lock and walked down the newly dried concrete path that led to the Manor. The master bathroom would be constructed as soon as it was approved by Rafe, but unfortunately for me, it was the last thing on his list as Alpha.

I knew Knox was on the prowl before he was next to me. His confused scent coated everything. His pace matched my own as he joined me on the walkway. He didn't say anything and the longer we stayed in silence, the more confused his scent became.

"What do you want, Knox?" My tone was soft but I was feeling anything but that. He was the absolute last person I wanted to deal with.

"How are you feeling?"

I stopped in my tracks and gave him a confused look. "Excuse me?"

He took a step away from me, which was probably a good thing. "Am I not allowed to care?"

I snorted. "Since when have you ever?"

"Since, always?"

I shook my head at him and kept walking. I could see Rafe's mom, Alice, watching us through the window and the last thing I wanted was an audience when dealing with this imbecile.

"Knox, I really don't have the emotional headspace for whatever you have to tell me or brag about. Can we do this emotional sparring on another day when I don't feel like the world is collapsing beneath me?"

He had stopped walking but I didn't care. "When are you going to talk to someone about the blame you are putting on yourself?"

I swallowed thickly as I opened the back door to the Manor. I wasn't that transparent. But he also didn't deserve my response.

"He's right, you know," Alice said from the hallway.

"I don't feel any blame," My words were too flat for my own liking.

"We can smell the remorse you're feeling."

I sighed before I closed my eyes briefly. "What do you want from me, Alice?"

"I want to help you feel better," She leaned against the wall and I finally caught sight of her outfit from the shadows. She was wearing long overalls with an olive long sleeve shirt under them. Her dark hair was braided away from her face. She looked ten years younger. "Rafe won't be approving the renovation on the cottage until you can participate in pack functions again."

I rubbed the back of my neck. "What kind of activities?"

"How is your wolf feeling?" Her questions were starting to irritate me.

She was feeling the same since the night everything had happened. She was feeling just as responsible as I was, but I couldn't admit it because once I did, the emotions would only get stronger. They would only get worse. I chose not to answer her question till she answered mine.

After a few seconds, she gave in. "You didn't run on the full moon."

I blinked as the realization hit me. She was right. My wolf hadn't fought to come to the surface.

She hadn't tried at all. In fact, I could hardly feel her now.

"Sometimes our grief and guilt will kill our wolves." Alice's words were a whisper but they echoed in my mind as if she had screamed them. Was I killing my wolf? "There is nothing that any of us can say to make this any better, but maybe, you need to talk to Rafe about this. If anyone is feeling terrible or if anyone should be, it's him."

I did the only thing I knew how to do, I ran. Away from her words and away from the pain flooding me. The only person that deserved to feel any sort of way was Rafe.

**CHAPTER 15**
JADE

After almost a week of Lucas sleeping on the floor, our guard finally brought another bed in. At this point, all I could think about was what sunlight felt like on my face again. One night I woke up to the smell of my mother's roasted tofu and I felt a feeling of homesickness I had never felt before. I had fallen asleep with a tear-soaked pillow.

On the sixth day, the guard opened the door and allowed us to walk around the compound we were being held prisoner in. Damian hadn't requested my presence again and I hadn't tried to seek him out. After the last conversation I had about him, I was left unsettled. Lucas didn't tell me any more of Damian's plans and I didn't ask. I didn't think I could handle much more. All I felt was sick. Would I ever get the chance to get out? Was this it?

The guard stayed close behind us but I no longer cared if he heard what we spoke about. If he had a wolf, as I expected, then he had heard everything else we had spoken about anyways.

"I miss my parents," I didn't know where the thought came from but as of late, it felt soul-crushing. I missed them more than I had ever missed them before. I hadn't missed them much on their trips because I had craved the peace of being alone. Now? With the thought of never seeing them again, I didn't know how to navigate this new emotion.

"I never thought I would miss mine," Lucas replied back quietly. He had been permitted a haircut earlier in the day and was now sporting short curlier hair. The scars on his neck were jagged and visible now. His eyes seemed to be clearer, not so sad. "I hated them once. That was why I went to live with other covens. My father didn't understand, but he had never understood who I was growing up. He had never tried to understand. I assumed he hated me and I wished I would have gotten answers before Damian got to me."

"How long has it been?" I couldn't imagine wondering if my parents loved me or not. I knew without a shadow of a doubt that they loved me more than anything else. They had showered me in copious amounts of love since I could remember. I had never felt like I needed to look for it anywhere else. That was why they were so confused over my love of partying and bad boys. I didn't have any kind of emotional trauma that explained it.

"Ten years,"

I stumbled. "Ten years since you have seen your parents?"

He nodded and the sadness entered his eyes. "And my sister."

"I don't have any siblings," I admitted.

"It is the worst and best thing that could have ever happened to me. See, my father loved my sister. She was everything I wasn't. But she was also kind and considerate. She loved me fiercely, even though she probably shouldn't have."

"How old are you?"

"Twenty-five," He chewed on the inside of his lip.

"You left when you were fifteen?" I couldn't imagine leaving my parents now, much less when I was younger.

He shrugged like it was no big deal. I didn't know what to say so we continued down the hallway in silence. After a few seconds, I realized we were walking in circles and we hadn't passed by a single person. I turned to our guard and scowled. "What's going on?"

"Damian thought it would be a good idea for you two to stretch your legs but didn't want you to get any ideas about escape. He had your hallway glamoured. You can walk and walk and walk but you will never get anywhere and you will never see anyone else."

Lucas snickered like he expected it.

Then it dawned on me. "If you are a witch, then why can't you get out of here?"

The look on his face broke something inside of me. "When the wolf was forced on me, it took everything with it. It took my hope, my dreams, my passions, and it took my magic too."

*And it almost took your life.* I couldn't keep my eyes from dipping to the scarring on his neck.

"How do you think your family would react to you having a wolf now?"

His face looked pained. "They would be overjoyed.

**CHAPTER 16**
JADE

Lucas and I were playing cards when the door to our room slammed open. We had been permitted some more luxuries. Luxuries I wasn't about to turn down. I was happy to have something to keep us occupied, rather than our thoughts and anxiety.

The guard today was different and I tried to keep the surprise off of my face. I couldn't let them know I had gotten attached to another person here. Having Lucas roped into this was bad enough.

"The man stays," The guard started. "Jade, you are to come with me."

I shrugged at Lucas before I followed the guard out. It was better to just go willingly, rather than fighting it. It could turn out to be something completely harmless.

I tried to remain positive, even though we both knew better. I was led down unfamiliar hallways until the man brought me to another public shower and locker room. Two women were waiting for me inside.

One of the women was lounging on a couch pushed into the corner of the room and the other was holding up a curling iron like it was an award. I took a step back before the blonde-headed woman jumped from the couch. The one with the hot tool in her hand just continued to watch me with bright eyes. Her hair was a light purple and something inside of me warned that she was a witch. It had nothing to do with her hair, or the way she looked but everything to do with her aura.

"I am Sheeva," The purple-haired woman smiled with all of her teeth.

The blonde wasn't nearly as happy or friendly. "I'm Bee,"

Sheeva continued talking like we were going to be great pals but I knew that wasn't going to happen. "Your presence has been requested by the Alpha of our local pack."

I frowned. "I thought Damian was the Alpha."

Bee barked out a harsh laugh. "He wishes he was an Alpha. He's nothing but wanna-be scum."

Sheeva threw a bobby pin at her and scowled at the both of us. "We have work we need to do or we will all be punished. This isn't the time to smack talk our oppressor."

*They hate Damian too.* I made sure to catalog that information for later.

Sheeva patted the chair in front of her and I gingerly sat down in it. She wasted no time before she started yanking my hair this way and that way. I didn't bother with watching what she was doing in the mirror. Instead, I kept my eyes on Bee. She was pulling an outfit from one of the lockers. My stomach clenched. It looked like something I had worn before everything had happened with Rafe. Before the change. It would have been an outfit I would have been excited to wear.

Now? Not so much.

Her light blue eyes met mine in the mirror. "You will not fight me. You will put this on."

My back jerked upright and I found myself standing. I walked over to her on numb legs. What was happening to me? My body was moving on its own accord. I jerked to a stop in front of her and then my body was returned to me.

"The magic that I have is at the disposal of Damian, if you do something I don't like, I will take your body from you." Her words were filled with a dark satisfaction but also, there was a note of sadness. She didn't like being able to do this but whatever Damian had over her was enough.

I looked at the floor. I had no idea what she was going through but I wouldn't make this harder than it had to be. I didn't want to be a prisoner either. I couldn't imagine what Damian had over her and I didn't want to know. It made this entire situation that much worse.

Modesty wasn't something I could afford here. I didn't bother with feeling embarrassed as I stripped the t-shirt dress over my head. The clothing that had been chosen for me didn't allow for underwear so I stripped it off just as quickly.

The clothes slid over my body in a new way. I imagined at one point they would have clung to my curves. But now there weren't many curves left. The little food I had allowed myself to eat had done this. My lack of transformations and running with Nalia hadn't helped. Tears filled my eyes to see my gaunt cheeks in the bright fluorescent lighting. Even my green eyes looked dull and lifeless. Whatever Damian was trying to sell, it wouldn't go well.

Sheeva seemed to sense where my thoughts had headed. "Nothing a little makeup can't fix." She patted the chair again, but this time she was more gentle. The strap of the black crop top fell down my shoulder and I tried to shrug it back up.

Once upon a time, I would have loved to have worn this and show off my cleavage but this time, I wanted to hide. Who was this girl and where was the real Jade?

## CHAPTER 17
JADE

My body was no longer my own. No matter how much I tried and fought against Bee's magic, there was no use. I couldn't do anything to break free from this hold. Was this what Cardan had experienced when his wolf was forced on him and then after his mind taken? Was this what Lucas had been put through too or had he been conscious? How hard had he fought it, knowing exactly what had happened to him?

My eyes stared straight ahead, even though I wanted to take in all of my surroundings. Bee stood on my left and Sheeva had disappeared. Damian was nowhere to be seen and now I wondered if he would actually make an appearance. I had been drugged again for us to leave the prison I had been held in. They hadn't tried the bag over the head trick this time, too afraid they would mess up my makeup and hair.

Bee's hand trembled against my arm but that was the only indication that she was nervous. My wolf senses were still gone but I wondered if they were back if I would be able to scent her anxiety in the air. I doubted it, Damian was too smart for that. My hand reached up and toyed with the curl laying over my shoulder. I fought it but it was no use. I was no longer in control.

Then I heard his voice and everything ceased to exist.

"She's here? She's safe?" Rafe's voice was pained. I fought the control being held over my mind. I couldn't see him but I knew he was close. We were at the edge of the woods but I didn't know where. A group of men stood behind me and I knew that one of them was the guard that had watched over my cell daily. I didn't know which, each of their eyes were bright gold now and they each had a similar build. I had zero allies here.

"Yes," Another male answered Rafe. I didn't recognize his voice. "She is safe and she wants to be here. Last I checked, she's unmated and she never pledged to a pack. What makes you think we are holding her here?"

*No.*

I fought Bee's control over my mind but all I could manage to get through was a blink and the jerk of my arm out of her grip. I watched out of the corner of my eye. She looked irritated but all she did was fold her arms over her chest.

"What kind of game are you playing?" Rafe's voice raised an octave as they grew closer.

My lips twitched against their will into a smile. Rafe broke through the tree line and came to an abrupt stop. His eyes weren't yellow this time. They were a deep chocolate brown. Not seeing his wolf so close to the surface had my heart doing a flip flop. What was he doing here? Was he here to save me?

"There is no game," The other man followed, behind him came the rest of the Guardians, but then my heart broke. The last one to come through was Tracey but she didn't look like the Tracey I had grown so close to in such a short period of time. Her eyes were hollow and her skin was pale. She no longer looked like the bronzed goddess I was used to. She looked worn out and exhausted, like she hadn't slept in months. When her eyes met mine, they filled with tears.

The smile stayed on my lips even as I fought and pleaded inside of my head for Bee to let me go. It was no use. My heart broke inside of my chest. How my body wasn't crying was beyond me. I had never felt such intense pain before.

One of the guards behind me stepped forward. "She is fair game. She was injured in the car accident and needed immediate attention. She chose to stay after what you did to her."

Rafe clenched his jaw but he didn't take his eyes off of me. I could see that he didn't miss a thing, especially how much weight I had lost. My body moved against my will again and I found myself pressed against the chest of the man behind me. His hand snaked around my bare stomach and dipped into the waistband on my mini skirt. Nausea swirled in my gut at the touch. I fought Bee harder, I screamed inside of my head until my body jerked forward and I fell to my knees. Mav leapt forward and helped me up. But it was no use, Bee was back in control. She made me jerk my arm away and snarl at him. It hurt. Everything hurt. Fighting her was making everything worse. Pain lit up the back of my neck and I knew if I continued, she was going to knock me out or worse.

I knew she was giving me the luxury of allowing me to see my friends again but it hurt too badly. I wished she had just taken control completely. Seeing them like this was too much. It was all too much.

*Coward.* Nalia whispered.

Finally, some relief coursed through me. She was still here. That was something. That was one kind of win. It gave me the little hope I needed.

"I am fine here, Rafe." My voice didn't even sound like my own. I practically choked on the words.

"Tell me if you're not safe, please, that's the only way we can help you." Rafe's voice broke as all the Guardians lined up behind him. Mav wouldn't look at me now. Tracey wouldn't either.

I sighed but it sounded garbled. *Good.* Bee's hold on me wasn't as strong as she thought. "I told you that I am fine, Rafe. You can leave now."

He smiled with all his teeth. "I don't think we will. We accepted an invitation to be among this pack. I think we will stay for a little longer." He looked at the man that hadn't spoken since they broke through the woods. He was a big burly man with a thick black beard. I had never seen him before. "Your little witch looks tired, Travis."

Bee's hand went to mine immediately and I was whisked out of there before anything else could happen. The guards had gone through whatever portal she had conjured too. One of them swore.

"Do you know what you did, Bee?" The one behind me growled. My body sagged forward and finally, I had complete control over my limbs again. My legs shook as I felt like I was forced back into them.

Bee leaned forward and put her hands on her knees. "She isn't like a typical wolf. She is stronger. My magic is depleted. Did you want her running to all of her friends?"

"Where's Damian?" I managed to get out.

Bee ignored me as she continued to speak to the guards. She had portalled us into a small house. I wobbled over to the couch in the living room. My body collapsed and I closed my eyes. My entire body felt weak. Was it because I had fought her so hard mentally and now I had nothing left to make my body function?

"You're right, but now they're going to be suspicious."

Bee collapsed on the couch beside me. "They

were already suspicious. I don't know this girl. How can I possibly portray her in the way her friends know her? It's easier when I'm trying to fool strangers. This takes too much out of me."

The blond man took a step toward us. He snarled. "Do you want your daughter to be punished? Must we replace you with a stronger witch?"

I could feel her tense beside me. No wonder she was here. I knew my parents would do the same. "Good luck finding someone more powerful than I am. Good luck finding someone you can blackmail. Every single coven in the United States is on lockdown. They know a threat is coming. The stones have told them of the darkness brewing."

## CHAPTER 18
RAFE

Something wasn't right. I couldn't smell Jade's wolf. I couldn't scent her anywhere on this property. The full moon hadn't been that long ago, I should have been able to scent her in the woods. But still nothing. I paced across the small cottage we had been allowed to stay in. Mav and Archer were squished onto the couch pressed against the wall. Tracey had disappeared in the kitchen and Knox, well there was honestly no telling where he had run off to. He was the one I worried about the most, but not because he was rowdy. No, I worried about him because he didn't know fear. He would run through this pack guns blazing if I allowed it. He would go through every single home looking for Jade if I said the word, consequences be damned. He was impulsive and reckless. He was my brother.

I squeezed my eyes closed as I listened to the other Guardians settle in around the house. They were sniffing for magic or anything else that would get us in trouble here. I pinched the bridge of my nose.

"She isn't herself," Mav's voice sounded pained. He loved Jade. He had cared for her the moment he had heard what I had done. Though I had offered them no explanation for my actions- I didn't have to- they treated me differently. None of them would understand, but that didn't matter. My redemption would come later, at the hands of Jade. I hoped.

"She's not eating," The words were difficult to get past my lips. Her clothes had hung off of her, instead of clinging to her. She had lost too much weight, her wolf had to be suffering. But I hadn't been able to scent that in the air around her either. Had they killed her wolf? It would explain how she was acting and the way she had lost muscle.

"They could be listening to us," Tracey whispered from the doorway to the kitchen. She held a bagel between her fingers but I doubted she was actually going to eat it. Tracey had lost weight too. She had hardly been eating. She had hardly seen the sun and her cheeks looked just as gaunt as Jade's had.

I straightened up and blinked slowly. I couldn't believe I hadn't seen it before. My desperation, my sadness, all of it... it was affecting the pack. I was killing my pack.

I gritted my teeth together. I had to give them hope. Hope that their future mates wouldn't be taken from them. Hope that their families would be safe. Hope that I would get Jade back and the pack dynamic would go back to normal.

"I don't care if they listen," I crossed my arms over my chest as a small smile stretched across my face. By the look on Tracey's face, it was my crazy smile. I didn't care. "In fact, I want them to know. I want everyone to know. I am willing to burn it all down for my mate."

Mav leaned forward and coughed. Knox clapped from the open doorway with a grin on his face. I knew he had been waiting for me to tell everyone else. Tracey had been the only one that knew. Her face paled further. Archer looked like he was ready to throw himself at me in a bear hug.

"I didn't want anyone to know why I fought so hard for her. I didn't want to share my failures as an

Alpha or as your friend. As your brother. I wanted you to have someone to look up to. I wanted my little brother to have someone to look up to but I threw that all away when I forced the change on her. I will not explain why I did what I did to any of you. Jade is the only person that I owe an explanation to, as my mate." I swallowed as all their eyes turned yellow. This was going to be a different fight now. This was personal. Jade was a part of our pack, whether she pledged to it or not. "I will burn down the entire world for my mate. Don't get it twisted. I would never hurt her intentionally. I would have never forced a change on her but time was running out."

Once again, Tracey was the only one that knew why I had done what I had. But it had taken me too long after the fact to explain it to her. Our friendship had suffered for it. I could see it in her eyes. The doubt that had festered there in the weeks she thought I was a terrible person. In the weeks she assumed I was insane and my wolf was making me sick. But as their Alpha, I owed them nothing. I owed them the protection of the pack and my strength, but I didn't owe them explanations for my actions.

Knox whistled and I sighed. "I was waiting for

this! I mean, we all assumed but you kept denying that you cared for her. *Finally.*"

I looked at each of the Guardians and they smiled slowly in turn. They had all known but had waited for me to tell them. Tracey still looked empty. I could smell Knox's confusion behind me.

"Tracey already knew," I admitted.

Knox lifted his lip in disgust. "You told her before *me*?"

I pinched the bridge of my nose again. Knox was going to give me a headache. "You were in training. Remember, zero communication with your past life?"

Knox pressed his lips together before he shot me a guilty grin. "Ahhh, right."

Tracey pushed past the threshold of the kitchen and sat on the edge of the couch that was occupied by two men that were entirely too big for it. "Plus, I can keep a secret. Unlike you idiots."

Mav frowned. "I would like to think that I am not included in that general term. You know how I hate generalization."

Tracey rolled her eyes but there was a ghost of a smile playing on her lips. She had a soft spot for the giant Samoan just like Jade did. He was like a big teddy bear, that could actually rip your face off if you wronged him.

Tracey leaned forward and watched me with determination. "You have our attention, Alpha. What's the plan?"

## CHAPTER 19
JADE

We hadn't gone back to the *main house* where I had been kept before with Lucas. My new home was with Bee, Sheeva, and two guards that I didn't recognize. We didn't speak and anytime I tried to, I got shut down. My only duty was to wear a bunch of different outfits during the day so the guards could take them off somewhere. I had a feeling it was to get my scent everywhere around this unfamiliar pack but I didn't ask questions. I just stared at the light gray walls around me. Dinner had been cooked at the main house but we weren't permitted to dine with the rest of the pack, though I knew that would really set Rafe off. He knew I needed a community, right? He would see through all of this.

I squeezed my eyes closed and rolled over. The

lights had been turned off for me but I had a little bit of night vision now. The pack here didn't cook their food in wolfsbane.

All that mattered was how long we had to put on this show. If I was here for a week, I knew I would get Nalia back. Would it be enough for me to escape, though? I pressed my palms into my eyes and thought of Rafe.

His hair was longer now. It was almost to his shoulders. He had pulled it back into a half bun on the top of his head. He wore black stud earrings and a plain long-sleeved shirt. He looked so casual and at ease, especially with his wolf tamed. What had happened while I was gone? Was it because I was gone? The Guardians had looked stronger than ever, I knew it was probably from overtime drills to prepare for whatever this mess was.

I sighed. Thinking of my friends would do me no good. Then I stopped and sat up. My hair fanned out around my face in a massive arc. *Friends*? When had all of them become that? The night of karaoke or before? I didn't know how this realization made me feel. I laid back down and pulled the blankets up to my neck. I cared for them, all of them. Even Rafe, just a *little* bit. I pressed my face into the pillow and let out a small sound of frustration. All I could do was hope. Hope that Rafe saw through all this mess or at least Tracey did.

"Get up," A voice whispered above me. I sat up abruptly and immediately regretted it as my head knocked into the one above me. He swore and I fell backward as pain unraveled in my forehead. I rubbed the tender spot as my eyes adjusted to the darkness. I must have fallen asleep pondering on everything that was going on with my pack. I blinked a few times before I attempted to sit up again. The pain was only getting worse. I pressed my palms into my eyes.

"What the hell is wrong with you?" I said wincing.

The man across from me, that I quickly recognized as my guard, held his bleeding nose. I would have smirked if we were in different circumstances.

"I was trying to be quiet but you ruined all of that." He swore again.

I exhaled hard before I scowled at him. "You were the one above me. It wasn't the other way around."

He leaned against the wall and pulled his hand

away from his nose. It was no longer bleeding. "I see your wolf is coming back."

I pressed my lips together.

"I came in here to help you,"

I couldn't have kept the laugh in even if I had tried. "Help?"

It was then that I noticed his icy stare. He was the guard that had been posted outside of my prison cell since the beginning. "Damian is getting antsy. You're going to have to be convincing to get your friends out of here."

My eyebrows scrunched together. "What does that mean?"

"Damian has been waiting for the moment that they would come sniffing around. He wants to kill them and this will give him the opportunity to do so." The guard's eyes watched the bedroom door. He wasn't supposed to be in here or telling me this. "So I need you to fight me."

My eyebrows shot up on my forehead. "Excuse me?"

"There are guards here that *want* you. They can smell your strength and potential as a mate, even if you smell of another. You need to fight me."

I still wasn't getting it. What did other guards have to do with this? Then before I could formulate any other thoughts or plans, he was on top of me. His teeth elongated and fear rushed through me. Before I knew what was happening his hands had mine pinned down. He pressed his nose to my throat and nausea hit me. "Scream."

I gritted my teeth together. "I will kill you."

He chuckled. "Good."

His teeth slid along my neck and Nalia perked up in my mind. *Hell no.* I kicked out and he flew across the room. Shock flashed across his face before he growled low in his throat. His feet skidded across the floor before he bumped into the wall. I shoved off of the bed and got into a crouching position. He wasn't going to take me so easily. Not again. Not ever. No one would ever take me again. I would kill them all. My teeth poked my bottom lip and fear washed over the room in a thick cloud.

The bedroom door banged open. Sheeva stood in the doorway with her hair a messy halo around her head and her skin pale. "What is going on in here?"

The guard straightened up and touched his nose, like I had just hit it. The blood still looked fresh, smelled fresh. But not to a witch's nose. She wouldn't know whether it happened now or an hour ago.

"The bitch hit me," The guard's eyes were bright yellow now.

Sheeva's eyes went between the both of us before they landed on me at last. "Are you okay?"

I shrugged my shoulders as I straightened up from my defensive stance.

Her eyes flicked back to my attacker. "What are you doing in here?"

When he smiled my blood ran cold. "Damian said we could take turns if we behaved. I figured it was my turn now. I have watched over her for weeks now. I'm getting really tired of waiting."

Sheeva's eyes grew wide. She bit her bottom lip before she nodded once. She wasn't going to help me. She was going to let them have their way with me if Damian said so? My lip lifted in a snarl. "Go clean yourself up." Her words were a command but her tone was anything but. Her voice shook as she folded her arms over her chest. I wondered if she was doing it to hide the trembling there too.

"I will do no such thing, I am going to bring her to Damian." The guard sneered. "He told me to bring her to him if she started to get out of line."

Sheeva's face went from scared to confused. "Damian is back in the Ro-" She stopped herself from revealing his location. "Damian is at least an hour's drive from here. If you take her off of the pack lands, the Crimsons will get suspicious."

The guard grinned. "Good thing Damian got here yesterday."

The color drained from Sheeva's face. "I wasn't prepared. I am still not prepared."

The guard pressed his lips together before he rolled his eyes. "Damian didn't want an audience. He came to see the girl here."

Sheeva nodded once. She wouldn't question the authority in front of her. "Be quick about it."

The guard stalked toward her, all swagger and danger in his body movements. "Keep this between you and me. There are certain things Damian does for himself. He doesn't want the pack here knowing what he is up to. If you gossip, I will make sure your family pays for it."

Sheeva nodded once before she fled the room. The man threw my shoes at me and didn't wait for me to dress before he wrapped his hand around my bicep and hauled me from the room. I recoiled from his touch all the way out of the cottage and to the tree line. He released me as soon as we were far enough away.

I stumbled a few steps before I contemplated running. "I'm sorry," his words came out choked and sad. I stopped walking and looked at him. His face wasn't full of overinflated confidence anymore. "I wanted you to pretend like you were fighting me but I could hear her in the hall, I had to do what I had to do in order to get you riled up."

It made sense. I should have listened but everything had happened so quickly, I didn't know what to believe anymore. There were traitors around every corner and I didn't know if there was a single person in this damned place that was willing to help me. Lucas was the only one but I still had my doubts about him. I couldn't trust so easily but now? I didn't have much choice tonight. I hung my head as we walked. This was all so heavy. I wouldn't be able to trust this guard until I saw my pack.

*My pack.*

Why hadn't I pledged to them when I had the chance? I could have prevented all of this. A tear slipped down my cheek and the guard beside me went ridid. "They know you're out here."

"Who?"

The word fell flat as Rafe's scent wrapped around me. My body sagged in relief. Tracey's scent was with him and then there was Knox.

"If you run with them, you'll make this harder on yourself and your pack." The guard whispered.

"He will kill my family too. He will slaughter this entire pack. I won't blame you if you go with them but this was simply to help them so they can fight again in the future. We want freedom and we need allies in order to get it."

All the planning I had been doing in my head to run came to a halting stop. He was right. Damian would kill every single person in this pack. He would do it as an example and then he would come back for me harder. He wouldn't stop until everyone I loved was dead. He would make sure I suffered for deceiving him. I squared my shoulders. I knew what I had to do, even if I didn't like it.

## CHAPTER 20
TRACEY

The woods told the secrets of the pack. They whispered to us as we walked through the trees and overgrown brush. There was so much to be learned in the places that the pack ran. A few wolves in this pack were sick and a few had been actively poisoned with wolfsbane. I ran my fingers over the rough bark on a tree before I heard it. A branch snapped in the distance.

We were being followed. I stopped and tilted my head to help me hear better. It was no use. There was magic here. It tainted everything in this pack. The sickly sweet smell coated everything. Even the grass slightly sparkled in it. A wolf wouldn't be able to see or smell it the way I could. The little part of my blood that held witch in it could identify what we were up against. I had seen the shimmering web of control wrapped around Jade the day before. The magic was strong and old. Telling Rafe wouldn't have helped us any either. He didn't know I could see the magical tethers in the world.

To be honest, I hadn't really known I could see it this well until we had stepped out of the car and onto this land. There were different kinds of witches in the world but they were all interconnected somehow. All of our blood was similar, even if our magic wasn't. I had always been around my grandmother's magic growing up. Seeing something like this was a shock. My granny's magic didn't coat everything like this. It didn't shimmer or sparkle. Something wasn't right about the magic and I couldn't say anything until I asked Granny about it. I was sure she would know. She had left her coven for a reason. I would need to know that too. *No more secrets.*

Secrets were what had gotten us into this mess. If only we had all been honest. But sometimes, honesty made everything worse. It was a massive tangled web that I so desperately wanted to get out of but I couldn't leave.

Knox twitched beside me. "She's here, but is this a trap?"

My ear twitched. I still couldn't hear anything. I wondered if it was the magic doing it. I didn't like it. The sickly sweet scent was starting to coat my mouth.

Rafe's eyes scanned the trees. "I don't think it's a trap, there is only one person with her."

"It could be a witch," The magic was starting to make me uneasy. The coating in my mouth made me feel sick and lightheaded.

Knox narrowed his eyes. "It's a wolf."

How were they able to scent all of this? How could they tell? All I could feel, taste, and smell was the magic in the air and on my skin. It was thick and toxic. It made my head swim. Granny's magic had never made me feel like this before.

I blinked a few times and then there she was. Jade stood in front of us but this time, magic didn't coat her skin. She wasn't tangled in the web of magic. I could barely smell her wolf. She was actually okay.

My head swam and I fought to stay upright. I needed to get out of this forest but not before we got Jade. Jade was all that mattered.

## CHAPTER 21
RAFE

Everything in my body tensed up, ready to fight but the man beside my mate simply put his hands up and took a step away from her. I rushed to her side and touched her face. She scowled at me and I realized that I had overstepped. I had revealed she was my mate to everyone else but her. "I'm sorry,"

Her eyes lightened and a smile tugged at the corners of her lips. "It's okay," Even her voice sounded normal now. It felt like a weight had been lifted from my shoulders. "But we don't have much time."

My eyes went to the man beside her. I recognized him as the man that had slid his hand into her skirt the previous day. I narrowed my eyes. I would never forget his face. The need to tear his head from his shoulders was strong. But I wouldn't start a war tonight.

"You're right," Tracey wobbled forward to grab Jade's hand. "We have to hurry if we are going to get you out of here and the rest of the Guardians." Her words sounded slurred now. Something wasn't right. My eyes went back to the guard at Jade's left. He had noticed Tracey was acting funny too.

I pointed at him with a clawed finger. "What do you know?"

The man's eyes didn't leave Tracey. "The woods are spelled against witches."

Tracey wasn't a witch though. My brows met and I turned to look at my friend just as she pitched forward and lost her footing altogether. Knox caught her with little effort. "She's not a witch, she's a wolf."

The man shook his head. "If she has witch blood inside of her, that's all this place needs. Anything that she touched here is poisoning her."

Knox looked pained as he held our friend in his arms. He was uncertain of what to do. Protect and get Tracey to safety or help me get my mate back. I shooed him with my hand. "Take care of her, I will be fine."

A growl rumbled through his chest. "I am not to

leave my Alpha. We should have brought more backup with us. This could be a trap."

The man took a step forward and held his hands up. "This isn't a trap but you will all die if you don't leave tonight."

Jade brushed Tracey's hair from her face as a tear rolled down her cheek. "He's right and that's why we are here. If you don't leave you will all be killed. If you take me with you or try to help me escape, the families in this pack will be hunted." She motioned to the stranger beside her. "His family and children will be slaughtered. I am not more important than all these people. It is our duty to protect them."

Everything in me screamed to tell her no. To tell her that she was my only priority. That the world could burn and I wouldn't give a damn as long as she was safe. That I was willing to let everyone die if it meant that she wouldn't. I would throw it all away and I knew it the moment I was willing to change her against her will. But I had a lot of redemption to earn and letting the world burn for her wasn't the way to get it.

## CHAPTER 22
JADE

I wasn't prepared for all the emotions that flooded me as I watched my friends walk away. A copper taste coated my tongue as I sharply bit down. I had never felt like I had wanted to go down on my knees and beg before, but I felt that as I watched them turn their backs on me.

"My name is Micah," the guard said as I watched them go. Tracey was completely limp in Knox's arms and Rafe didn't look back once. I had seen the internal war going on in his eyes as I told them to leave. I had seen the struggle he had within himself to allow me to stay behind but I didn't care. I had to be firm and crying would do none of us favors. Running away with them would do nothing for the people here.

My chest ached as I thought of my parents and what they were going through. Or what they would go through if this didn't go well for me. I squeezed my eyes closed before I turned to the guard beside me. "It's nice to meet you, Micah."

The tightness in my chest bloomed into something I wasn't prepared for. I struggled to breathe as I realized, once again I was alone. I was going to have to do all of this by myself and there was a possibility I wouldn't find out how Tracey fared. I pressed my palm to the center of my chest and blinked rapidly to try to clear the tears from my eyes.

"Who's side are you on?" The words came out barely a whisper as I ducked my head and turned back toward the cabins.

"I hate to break it to you," Micah's voice went hard. "But I do have to bring you to Damian now. It wasn't a lie. He is waiting to see if you have tried to escape or if you are going to. The fact that your friends are packing up to leave now will be a good sign."

I pressed my lips together. "That doesn't answer my question."

"The answer to that is a bit more complicated." He hung his head. "I wish I could give up all of my secrets, but for right now, I have to escort you to Damian and he's already going to be suspicious enough."

Damian leaned against a blacked-out Mercedes parked on the edge of the empty highway. When he noticed I wasn't blindfolded he narrowed his eyes.

Micah shrugged like it wasn't a big deal. "I could hardly parade her around her friends with a sack over her head."

Damian lifted an eyebrow as he smoothed his hands over an old band tee. "Your friends? They still haven't left."

I cocked my head to the side with indifference. "They're leaving now."

Damian's eyes flicked to Micah's. "Is this so?"

"Yes, we ran into them on the way out. They are leaving now."

Relief and surprise flashed across Damian's face. "You were that convincing?"

"I just told them what they needed to hear. I didn't want to go back there and I didn't want to see them anymore. I don't think you'll have to worry about them sniffing around again." I shrugged even though it hurt to speak the lies.

Damian steepled his fingers under his chin. "That's interesting. You want to stay here?"

"Under a few conditions," I picked at my nails in mock boredom. He nodded for me to continue. "No more witch shit. No more invading my mind, mind control, or anything like that. I will be here willingly or wherever you want me to go, but I won't be controlled."

Damian's smile caused a chill to skitter down my back. "We had to make sure you would be loyal, that you wouldn't try to run. This worked better than I thought it would."

"How is Lucas?" I didn't care for the small talk anymore. I wanted to know how my friend was. I had my suspicions that he was being mistreated with me gone.

"He is boring," Damian bared his teeth. "All he does is sit in your room and play cards with himself."

That seemed strange. Why would Lucas play cards with himself? I wanted to look at Micah but I couldn't give myself away. I couldn't let him know I had an ally in this mess. He had to believe I was all in, on my own. Friends would come later.

Damian pushed off of the edge of the car and patted Micah on the shoulder. "I thought I would have trouble with you, especially after your first few months here. I'm glad to see you are finally accepting the cause."

Micah nodded. "I wasn't thinking clearly before. The wolfsbane will do that to you."

Damian smiled again, but wider this time. "Good, glad to hear it. Gather the group that is waiting back in the cabin then head back to HQ. It's time Jade met the rest of our rogues."

## CHAPTER 23
TRACEY

Shouting blasted me from the sweet darkness that had wrapped around my consciousness. I blinked my eyes slowly as the lights berated me from above. I tried to throw my arm over my face to shield me from the abrasiveness, but it was no use. My arms wouldn't corporate. I kept my eyes closed even though it wasn't much relief from the brightness around me.

"For all I know, she hasn't had witch blood. Usually, one species takes over the other and destroys it. She shouldn't be having this kind of reaction." My granny's voice was shrill. "She has never shown signs of knowing magic before. As far as I knew, the magic lay dormant in her DNA. There aren't many wolf/witch babies out there.

Normally shifters mate with other shifters, not other supernatural species. It should have been impossible for them to have one child, and they managed to have two. This is all new to me."

I had never heard Granny so panicked before. Another person spoke beside her and it took me a moment to recognize Carden's voice. I had forgotten he still lived here with her. He was a prisoner for a while but now, all he wanted to do was learn about magic and help Granny. I didn't understand it but I also hadn't had time to ask questions while I had been knee-deep in cottage renovations. "Do you think you could contact the covens around here and see if they know anything about it?"

Granny clucked her tongue. "I'm afraid not, boy. Witches did this and they would not be so fond to help. There is more to this than what appears. We can't risk our stance. We have a witch and a wolf in one body. The last thing we need is to get Pack Law involved, or the other covens. This could be more dangerous than what we are already dealing with."

With that, I let out a groan as I tried to roll over. I didn't know where I was but I was tired of being talked about like I wasn't lying right there next to them. Hands grasped me as I went airborne, right off of the table they had me perched on. No wonder my body ached the way it did. They had me on a metal exam table.

"Turn the damn lights off please," My voice croaked out from a dry throat. I coughed once before it felt a little better, then a glass was being pressed to my lips. I couldn't remember what had happened last. I remembered seeing Jade.

I shot up and almost collided with Knox. He was the one pressing the cup to my lips. My head swam with the sudden movement. With trembling hands, I managed to take the cup from the Guardian's fingers. He tried to give me a reassuring grin but all it did was the opposite. Who had hounded him to care this time?

Rafe had his hands braced on either side of the wooden chair. It was flipped around so he straddled it. His hair was pulled back slightly and his eyes were dark, but not with his wolf. "Good morning, sleeping beauty. How was your rest?"

I scrunched up my nose. "It was fine, as long as none of you woke me with a kiss." My eyes found Knox's right before he smirked. My look went lethal. He held his hands up in surrender before he chuckled. The dark sound wrapped around me and I felt myself shiver in response. I clamped down my teeth and tried to not rip him apart. Damn him, and damn the rest of them. I didn't need an audience as I had awoken.

"How are you feeling?" Granny's voice ripped me from my rage. When I looked up at her I blinked. Golden threads wove around her in intricate patterns. They never stopped moving. It reminded me of the forest before I had seen Jade. I blinked then blinked again but it didn't matter. The gold remained around her like she was an angel.

Granny's eyes softened as she watched something shimmering around me. I held my hands up to inspect myself but there was nothing there. "You can't see your own magical aura. I would imagine that's what you're seeing around me now."

I nodded my head uncertain. This was new territory for all of us, based on their conversation.

"It wasn't until you were conscious again, that your aura flared to life. You can prevent people from seeing it as you learn more about witchcraft. But for now, this is very interesting." Granny got down on her knees and before I knew it, I was pulled into one of her amazing hugs. Relief and love flooded my body. If anyone knew how to help me navigate all of this, it was Granny. "I will recommend that you don't leave the Pack Lands until you get this under control. You have a lot to learn before we release you back into the big world with witches that will want to dissect you."

I nodded my head. I could agree to that, it would cause more trouble than it was worth if I ran into another witch or I insisted on helping with Jade and only made things worse. After all, I was probably one of the main reasons we had to leave so quickly the other night and I probably put Jade in danger.

I looked up at Rafe and smiled. "Where is Jade? I figured she would be here when I woke up, but I kind of understand. She looked like she needed a lot of rest and food. Just tell me you didn't show her the cottage yet."

The Alpha and Knox shared pained looks. Rafe spoke first. "She isn't here."

He didn't elaborate and I didn't know if it was for my sake or for his. Granny took that as her cue to explain it to me. "There were a few complications besides the magic spelled against you."

I didn't know if I wanted to know. "How am I still here if I was poisoned?"

Knox scratched the top of his head. "You have your wolf to thank for that. She saved your life with your advanced healing."

That made sense. "They're holding her prisoner." I had to know, even if I didn't want to.

Rafe clenched his jaw. "They are holding a lot more than her prisoner there."

"Then why don't we bust up in there and save them?" Carden said from the doorway. It was so weird to see him innocent and without all the piercings and tats that he had before. The spell had seemed so realistic.

Knox sighed. "Their pack is highly protected. Whoever is being held captive, isn't there."

"She didn't tell you who is holding her prisoner?" I couldn't believe what I was hearing.

Knox chewed on his lip. "We didn't exactly have time for questions."

*Oh*. Because of me.

## CHAPTER 24
JADE

"I want to be able to call my parents." We were blasting down the highway faster than I had ever gone. I was too scared to take a peek at the speedometer. A heart attack was imminent if I knew. I closed my eyes and leaned back in the seat.

*Ignorance is bliss.*

"I don't know if that's a good idea," Damian said from the driver's seat. I didn't bother opening my eyes to look at him. I would die on this hill.

"I told you that I would be willing to work with you, now I expect you to do the same." I felt myself wanting to pout. My bottom lip started to pucker before I sucked it into my mouth. None of that. I couldn't afford to get comfortable. I couldn't afford for him to think I was flirting. I shivered.

"You don't think your parents will want to see you?" He scoffed.

"Magic is a powerful force, I understand but you need to understand that eventually they are going to want to see me. Is your game a long one?" I opened my eyes and leveled him with a death stare.

He let out an exasperated sound. "Yes, relatively."

"Then they will come looking. I don't know how much you looked into me before you made your plans, but my parents fought to have me. They have hovered my entire life. All I know is them. If you don't let me speak to them or see them, they will get suspicious and then your operation will crumble to the ground."

He didn't say anything back and I let him stew on it. There was no point in continuing to try to sell it. We had already been in the car for what felt like hours. I hadn't realized where we had been playing pretend was so far from where we actually stayed. I didn't even know what to call it. The compound? HQ? Hell?

As he pulled down a long winding dirt road, his eyes turned toward me. "Fine, you can call your parents and possibly see them. But you'll have to tell them the same thing you told the Crimson Pack. You'll have to explain you've taken up work somewhere else, or that you are required to travel because your boss wants you as his right-hand man." He winked. "You can possibly twist it into a workplace romance if you'd like, if you think it'll sell it. I don't care."

Hope flared brightly in my chest. Before I could stop myself, I threw my body across the little space separating us and wrapped my arms around him the best I could. "Thank you!"

His body tensed before he relaxed a bit and I had to remind myself that he was the villain here. That he had kidnapped me. But something in the back of my head reminded me that Rafe had still turned me without my consent. That was where the lines got blurred and I knew, if I wasn't careful, I would fall right into the belly of the beast without any way out.

🐾

Lucas was waiting in my room with a deck of cards. He was flicking through each card when I opened the door. To the common, untrained eye they looked just like regular playing cards. But as I got closer, I noticed something different on the faces of each card. It was a tarot deck. I grinned. I wondered how he had managed to get that in here or if Damian was experimenting with the once witch.

He didn't look up when I sat across from him. I had brought in a whole trove of clothes with me, except they weren't for me. They were for him. He didn't look up. His bronzed fingers worked through the deck of cards once more.

"You've been gone for a while," His voice held no emotion as he shuffled the deck.

"I brought you back a gift," I nudged the suitcase beside my foot.

He continued playing with the cards. "You sold your soul to the monster."

I felt my lips stretch across my teeth in a predatory grin. "Lucas, the only monster I sold myself to, was myself. I might not have been monster material before, but I sure as hell am now."

His eyes flicked up to mine before they looked over my body. "What did they do to you?"

I leaned forward like I was going to kiss his neck but instead whispered into his ear. "They showed me the one thing I am willing to fight for."

He leaned back and planted his hands on either

side of himself. His cards forgotten now. "What's that?"

I ran the tip of my tongue over my canine. "Myself, silly."

## CHAPTER 25
JADE

The sound of the phone ringing was like music to my ears. I had never thought it possible to miss my parents as much as I did but when my mother's voice blasted through the speaker my chest got tight. My eyes burned as I tried to think of what to say. I had been able to read all the text messages between my parents and the fake Jade. I had a little insight on the role I was supposed to play.

"Two calls in one week!" My dad's voice sounded thrilled. I pressed my palm to my chest as an unfamiliar feeling washed through me. "We must be super lucky! What do we owe the occasion?"

"I just missed you," My voice broke and I knew when my mom caught onto my emotion immediately.

"Are you okay?"

I closed my eyes and sighed. "Of course, I'm just a bit homesick. I don't think I have ever been away from home this long before. Do you ever feel like this?"

"Yes, sweetie!" My mom reassured me. "We feel that way often. Especially without you here when we get back. When do you think you'll be coming home? You said you're going to finish school remotely?"

I swallowed hard. I didn't want to lie to them but I knew I had no other choice. They couldn't be put in danger. They were so fragile. I couldn't risk it. "About that," I paused as I gathered my thoughts. "I'm going to be traveling for a while. I was offered a new position recently and well," This was the part I hated the most. "I started seeing someone."

My dad chuckled as my mom spoke. "I knew it! I knew there had to be something more keeping you away like this!"

"Tell us all about him," My dad didn't sound amused at all and I knew he only asked to humor my mom.

My thoughts immediately went to Rafe. The

way his hair had fallen across his collar in the woods. The constant smirk he wore on his face. The golden hue of his eyes when I first met him.

But it wasn't Rafe I described. "He's very headstrong and has an incredible work ethic. He's a big team leader and he loves to play games." *Mind games.* "He's very handsome and determined." None of it was a lie, but not exactly the truth either.

"We can't wait to meet him. What's his name?" My mom wasn't going to let me skimp on any details.

"Damian," I breathed.

Lucas's eyes shot to mine from across the room. I didn't know why I had thought today would be a good day to call them but I couldn't put it off any longer. It wasn't like I could leave this room and I definitely couldn't kick Lucas out either.

"Ohhhh," my mom cooed into the phone. "I already know you have good taste too! I'm sure he's just as good looking as the rest of the men that would frequent the house."

My dad let out an exasperated sound. "On that note, I think we are going to be late for our train."

They were in Belgium again, I had read in the text messages. Dad had a huge client that lived there. He liked to do freelance accounting for rich people all over the world. At least that was what he said. There was no telling what he really did. He was technically retired and had invested right. But he was a workaholic and there was no telling how he was managing to scratch that itch now.

After a few goodbyes, they hung up and I was left with silence on the other end. It took me a few moments before I could pull the phone away from my face.

"So that's how it's going to be?" Lucas leaned against the wall now and his eyes practically glowed in the dim lighting. He wasn't happy.

"What?"

"Damian and you," He growled through gritted teeth.

I rolled my eyes. "I have to do what I have to do to keep them safe. I would never sell my body like that."

"And what if that's what he requires next?"

I thought of the night Knox had ripped the heart from the rogue's chest. The night I had thought he was a horrible person. I had been terrified but now? I couldn't help but smile. "Then I will enjoy ripping his heart from his chest. Nalia will enjoy eating it."

The yellow in Lucas's eyes faded. "You think you are up for that challenge?"

I shrugged my shoulders. "I don't know but I will say this. Do not underestimate me, unless you want to die too."

"You aren't the scared pup they threw in here weeks ago."

"Good."

🐾

I didn't know what game Damian was playing at but our meals were no longer laced with wolfsbane and we didn't have a guard posted at our door anymore. But I knew better than to think the surveillance in our room had been turned off. I knew we were being watched even if someone wasn't posted at the door and I knew better than to think they didn't know our every move if we left the room.

Lucas shook his head the first day we had left our room. He hadn't wanted to go. He insisted it was a trap but they hadn't brought us a meal and I was starving. I could keep myself from eating a lot but I needed something. The water from the shower didn't keep my stomach full. So I shrugged and yanked the door open. I blinked a few times when I realized Micah wasn't at the door. Then I shrugged again and left. Lucas whispered aggressively behind me as I walked away and found the cafeteria.

It wasn't as busy as it usually was and I wondered if they were using us as a social experiment. No one looked up as we passed, like they usually did. We were allowed to get our own food and it actually smelled like real food. When the lady on the other side of the counter passed me a massive slice of chocolate cake, I felt like I was going to cry. My nose immediately started to burn and my eyes filled. I doubted she was doing it out of kindness, but the fact was, I couldn't remember the last time I had had something sweet. Maybe at the Crimson Manor? But how long ago was that? All of my days were blurred together at this point.

Lucas looked equally emotional and shocked as she gave him a slice even bigger than my own. The edges of the icing grazed over the side of the white plate. He didn't wait till we got to the table and didn't even use a fork. He simply stuck his mouth right into the top of it while he managed to balance his tray full of other mouthwatering foods. It wasn't until we sat down that he pulled his mouth away from the dessert.

His entire mouth and chin were covered in chocolate icing. He grinned at me lazily as he picked up a fork and ate the rest of the cake before his actual lunch. How long had he been here? When was the last time he had eaten like this or enjoyed his food? I pushed my cake to him as guilt flooded me. He had been here a lot longer than I had. He deserved all the cake.

Country fried steak sat untouched on my tray but not for long. The scent of it was driving me crazy, almost as crazy as the cake. All of our food was gone in seconds. We wolfed it down without really tasting anything. Lucas ate both slices of cake before he finished off his lunch too.

"You're going to have a tummy ache," I teased.

He rubbed his flat belly as he wiped the cake from his face. "Completely worth it." His eyes darkened as he realized something. "You didn't have to give me your dessert."

"And miss you eating more than three grown men? I don't think so. *That* was worth it."

His eyes sparkled. I watched him as we put our empty trays on the garbage cans and walked back to our room. I didn't want to test how far we could go. We would try another day. Lucas had a new pep in his step as we went down the hall. If chocolate cake could do that, what else would make him elated?

We didn't speak as we neared our room. There was a healthy silence between us. Both of us full and satisfied with the turn of events through this captivity. I knew better than to grow to like it. I wasn't naive to think Damian wasn't dangling a prize in front of my nose. He would rip it away as soon as he saw fit.

I almost groaned when the smell of chocolate cake hit my nose. What torture. I couldn't believe he still smelled like it. That was until we turned on the light and I noticed the slice of cake sitting on the table beside my bed. I unfolded the note slowly as I felt the same burning I had before.

*You put others before yourself. It doesn't go unnoticed. You have a friend in the cafeteria if you ever need anything.*

Disappointment slammed into me as I realized I hadn't gotten a good look at the woman's face. But that was gone as soon as I dug into the cake and the chocolate coated my tongue. Maybe captivity wasn't so bad as long as I was protecting others. I didn't like to play games but I knew I had to risk it all with children involved. Bee and Sheeva both had families stuck in the middle of this. I was sure Lucas did too. Why else was he here?

I licked the spoon and sat the empty plate down outside the door of our room. Lucas was singing in the shower when I pulled the blankets up around my legs. It was time I got some answers from him on why he was here. It was only fair.

## CHAPTER 26
RAFE

Axel watched me with his dark eyes. Now that the secret was out of the bag, he didn't seem as angry with me.

"This could have been prevented," He didn't sound stern but disappointed. "She could have been protected if you had let me know."

"Let you know and risk something happening to her if you aren't on my side?" I crossed my arms over my chest. My wolf was docile in my head. Since I had outed our biggest secret and accepted Jade as my mate, he had calmed down. He no longer felt like I was fighting that part of myself. Wolves were weird.

Axel ground his teeth together and the sound made me cringe. I rolled my shoulders back as I prepared for the reprimand I knew was coming. "I am always on your side, just like I was on your father's but things are changing and you aren't the same Alpha he was. I can't continue to treat you like a child. I should have trusted your judgment."

I lurched forward in surprise. I swore my brows shot through my hairline. "Wait, what?"

Axel chuckled as he leaned forward at his desk. "You never treated Tracey any different for the dominant wolf inside of her and you still haven't treated her differently now with the magic. You have always been a good friend to my kids," His voice broke on the last word. Tracey's brother had been missing for years and we all knew it was intentional. He hadn't been loved in this pack like Tracey had been by me and the Guardians. The rest of the pack wasn't as forgiving or progressive when it came to his sexual preferences. Tracey had insisted he not come out to the pack, but he had done it anyway. She had wanted to protect him while he needed to live his truth. "I should have trusted you but seeing your wolf so close to the surface when you are the calmest out of all of us… it set me on edge. I was afraid you not finding a mate was causing you and your wolf to go mad with it."

I nodded my head. I could understand that. I

had worried myself in those moments. My mind had gone to a dark place when I had smelled the sickness in the air that night. "I can see why you were worried, I was worried too."

Axel stood up from the desk and patted me on the shoulder. "You are a good leader to our people. I'm sorry I didn't see it before. We will get your mate back, but it's not going to be a pretty fight."

My gums ached as my canines elongated past my lips. "I prefer to fight dirty, Axel. You should know this by now."

All he did was grin and this time, it met his eyes.

Knox met my stride as I left the main house. He had gotten a ridiculous haircut the previous day and I couldn't stop looking at it. What had he been thinking? His hair was just barely past his shoulders and he had shaved off the sides of his head right above his ears. He looked like he had a mullet and a Mohawk at the same time. Tracey had about had a heart attack when she saw it before she couldn't stop laughing. It was the only thing that had gotten a good emotional response out of her in days. He had it in a little bun at the back of his head and I wondered, as I looked at him, if he had done it for that reason.

Today he was in his fighting leathers and bringing that up wasn't a part of the itinerary. Jokes couldn't be brought to the war room. If we didn't stay serious we would lose our advantage on all of it. Whoever had Jade didn't know what we knew. He or she didn't know that we left to keep people safe. They probably thought we were going quietly with broken hearts. Little did they know we were going to start a war.

Tracey rounded the corner with a little smile on her face. It was the first time I had ever seen her in fighting leathers, and apparently Knox too because his eyes about fell out of their sockets at the sight. I averted my eyes politely but smacked Knox on the back of the head anyway. We couldn't be distracted. There were too many people at stake.

The war room wasn't one that my father used often. My father had used it as a private study and my mother had never been permitted inside. Even though he had loved her fiercely, he had always said this place wasn't a place for love. It was a place to plan, a place to fight for love and justice. If the men couldn't keep it together over the woman I knew would be my second someday, then they wouldn't be permitted to participate.

The only reason Tracey wasn't my second now was because she refused to challenge her father over the title. But we all knew she outranked him and the other wolves in the pack. I didn't mind her waiting, now that I knew where Axel stood in all of this, I rested easier. He had chosen to sit out of this meeting, he wanted his daughter there in his place. He would probably end up stepping down so she didn't have to challenge him for the place. I could practically smell it in the air. All Axel wanted was for his daughter to do great things and he knew that he was in the way of that.

I stopped at the massive utility building that looked nothing more than a place to hold heavy equipment. The metal walls were dull with age but the thick wooden doors in front of me were bright and shiny like they had been polished recently.

I turned to my Guardians and Tracey. I placed a hand on the door reverently. "This is a place we go to fight for our love. Love isn't permitted in here. Lust isn't allowed. If you can't keep your actions platonic while we are in this room, you will be asked to leave. I trust that you all have had the proper training to be here and know when to be serious and when to joke around. I trust all of you or you wouldn't be here with me."

I shoved the double doors open. The smell of whiskey and tobacco wrapped around me. I closed my eyes for a moment to let the nostalgia pass over me. Emotions would cloud my judgment and I didn't need them to hinder me any more than they already had. I should have come here alone before this, but there was no one else I wanted to experience this with.

I had only been in this room once. It was the night before I killed my father and took his place as Alpha.

**CHAPTER 27**
JADE

Pancakes were usually my favorite. Especially when they were slathered in as much butter as I could get on them. Growing up in a vegan household made me appreciate the finer things in life.

AKA butter.

But today, I couldn't stomach them. I couldn't bring myself to eat one bite. I shoved my tray away from me and watched with sickening fascination as Lucas devoured twelve pancakes and three cinnamon rolls. I couldn't keep the grin off of my face as he finished off his second glass of orange juice.

He stopped mid-sip. "What?"

"One would think you haven't eaten in years,"

He set the glass down hard and the juice sloshed over the side of the rim. His eyes went cold as he shoved his, now, empty tray away from him. "Maybe I haven't."

I leaned forward on my crossed arms. "I wouldn't know."

He narrowed his eyes. "What do you want to know, Jade?"

"How long have you been Damian's prisoner?"

He pursed his lips together. "That's a complicated answer."

I cocked an eyebrow. If we were going to continue on like this, I had to trust him. Yes, I know about his family somewhat but I didn't know why he was here. He still knew too much about me. I needed a friend but I was too afraid of getting close to someone here. What would it do to me? It would destroy me if I allied with the wrong person.

He sighed before he leaned forward. "I fell in love with Damian five years ago," My heart stopped. He grabbed our trays before he held a hand out to me. I placed my hand in his hesitantly then he yanked me from the table. He looped his arm through mine as we walked. "We met in a coven during a sacred holiday. I thought he was a gift from the gods. I thought he was everything I had been waiting for. But he didn't love me. He was looking for witches to aid him in his cause. He brought me back to his hotel room and I thought it was finally going to be my night, the night that everything was going to change. He jabbed a needle into my neck after he got me down to my underwear. Later he admitted it was in case I transformed immediately. He didn't know what would happen, I was his first witch changed wolf. I was the first of his experiments."

The burning returned in the back of my eyes. I couldn't breathe as he continued to speak.

"I thought he was the sun and the moon, turned out he was only a man. An evil man that couldn't turn himself so he sought out to destroy others." He chuckled but the sound was flat. "He held me captive and away from others for five years. When they threw you into my cell, I didn't know what to make of it. I still don't."

"He's kept real meals from you this entire time?"

Lucas nodded his head. "Yes, after I tried to rip his throat out when I realized what he had done to me."

It took me a few minutes to realize Micah was at our door. Now that I knew who he was, he no longer wore a ski mask. His lips twitched a bit when my eyes met his. I narrowed my eyes at him. He had helped me but I wasn't sure if I could trust him either. I pinched the bridge of my nose. All of this was making my head hurt. If I was going to beat Damian I had to be ten steps ahead but he was five years ahead of me, possibly more.

"Good morning, Micah," I cocked my head to the side in a greeting.

"Damian is requesting your presence," His voice didn't sound entirely happy about it and Lucas stiffened beside me. I pulled my arm from his and Micah held out his elbow like a true gentleman. What was going on here? Somehow I had gone from the prisoner to the princess.

Damian was waiting for me in a lavish sitting room on the other side of this jail. I wasn't entirely sure what to call it all yet but it certainly wasn't a palace, even if Damian's rooms suggested otherwise. He stood up from his chair and practically glided to me. I felt Micah's hand tighten briefly, in warning, on my arm before he released me to the beast.

"I hope you have been enjoying all the extras lately." Damian wrapped his fingers around mine and pulled me to a balcony that overlooked the mountains. There were two white rocking chairs to the left of us. He sat down in one before he motioned for me to sit in the other.

"Yes, the chocolate cake has been delicious," I motioned down to my white shirt and jeans. "Having actual clothing is also a bonus. We no longer stick out like sore thumbs when we leave our room."

Damian faced me with zero emotion on his face. I didn't like that I couldn't read him. What was he playing at? "Lucas told you about me."

I kept the surprise off of my face at the change of topic all of a sudden. I didn't know why I was surprised to begin with, he had eyes and ears everywhere. Of course he knew.

I nodded my head. "Yes, he did."

Damian leaned back in his chair and rubbed his chin thoughtfully. "I would love to tell you that I'm not a monster. I would deny the claims if they weren't true. But they are."

I kept my eyes on the mountains while he spoke. I couldn't bring myself to look at him, I knew if I did this entire charade would come crumbling down around me. I had to remain stoic. I rubbed my hand over my mouth before I allowed myself to talk. Like the action would keep me from revealing all of my secrets.

"Why would you do that to him?" My voice broke. There was no denying the hurt in my voice. There was also no point in hiding it. But what I couldn't do was attack him with my hands or my words. I had to be diplomatic about this.

"He was the perfect specimen," He chuckled like he knew a secret I didn't know. "Born of wolf shifters but having no wolf."

Chills ignited along my arms. That's what Lucas had meant when he had said his family would be delighted. He was more witch than he was wolf. I looked at Damian as something started to dawn on me. The corners of his lips quirked up.

"He wouldn't tell you who they are, but I have a feeling you already know. He knows who Rafe Crimson is, little wolf. Rafe is the one that protected him from all the others."

I pressed my palms into the tops of my thighs. It was the only thing I could do to keep myself from flying across the space between us. It all made sense. He had shackled me to Tracey's brother. But was it to torture me or to torture Lucas? And what of

Rafe? He had protected Lucas? Why hadn't Lucas said anything?

"He tried to kill himself, did he tell you that?"

I nodded stiffly.

"All this time his family has thought he has stayed away willingly." He rubbed his hands together like he had won a larger prize than Rafe Crimson's head. I couldn't imagine how he would act if he got that. "I originally planned to kill him after letting him live this way for five years. Can you imagine living in your own filth for five years? I'm surprised he still has a wolf anymore, he has had so much wolfsbane pumped into him."

Blood roared through my ears as I tried to fight the urge to rip him to shreds. I tucked my hands together as I peeked claws breaking through the tips of my fingers.

"Wouldn't it be fun to tell him how she's a witch now? Oh, how the tables have turned."

My head snapped up. He knew she was a witch now?

"I scented her change in the woods after you convinced them to leave. It's funny how powerful magic and powerful emotions can override everything else."

Then something else clicked into place.

"She was a social experiment too?"

He smiled and his face transformed into something beautiful. Something deadly. "Oh yes. You see, Lucas still has his magic shimmering under there somewhere. His wolf didn't destroy it like I hoped it would.

## CHAPTER 28
TRACEY

The food on my plate smelled good. It was my favorite, after all. My mom had gone through the trouble of cooking up an entire southern comfort meal for me. They had hoped it would help bring me back to myself. But as I stared down at the food, I didn't feel like myself. I could still see the magic around us shimmering softly. Granny had confirmed that this was how the witches saw the world. Everything was interconnected by the strands of magic. The first few hours had given me a headache and Granny had insisted that I would get used to it. Eventually, I would be able to block it out completely and see the world normally again. But it would take years of concentration and practice. Years I didn't have.

"How long have you known Jade was Rafe's mate?" My father scooped up a massive serving of mashed potatoes and plopped it onto his plate before he moved onto the gravy beside it.

I looked down at my own untouched potatoes. "I have known since Rafe knew."

The fork in my mother's fingers clattered to her plate. "Really?"

I shrugged. "I don't know why it's such a big deal. I don't know why you're surprised. Rafe and I have been best friends since we were children. He is the only one that accepted the dominant wolf under my skin. He's the one that invited me into his band of misfits and trouble."

My dad smiled as he cut into his chicken. "We absolutely shouldn't be surprised, you're right. But I wish you would have told me. I could have helped."

I pushed the potatoes around my plate. "I will not betray my Alpha or his trust."

"Yes, but I could have accepted the fallout from everyone else. I could have helped the pack accept it, rather than fuel the raging fire it became."

"You're perfectly happy with the way things are now, now that he told you she's his mate?" I set my fork down carefully beside my plate.

"Why wouldn't I be? We should be celebrating."

He grabbed my mother's hand and tucked it inside of his massive one.

"He changed her against her will, did everyone forget about that?" I was on Rafe's side until that had happened. I had agreed that he needed to get to know her. I had agreed that I would find out everything there was to know about Jade, but he had still violated her. He acted against her and didn't care about her consent. I understood why but I doubted my father did.

My father sighed. "What is done, is done. That is his mate, he has every right to do what he did."

I leaned back in my chair and barked out a laugh. "Are you still living in the dark ages? He doesn't own her."

This was why I never wanted a mate. I would never be owned by anyone, regardless of what *fate* said.

My father chewed his food for a minute while my mom looked at her plate submissively. They had a good, healthy relationship. I had adored learning from their example as I grew up but something wasn't right about this. Wasn't my mom going to stand up to him? I had seen her do it before. Unless she agreed with him…

"Mom?"

She sighed this time. "What do you want me to say? I don't agree with the part that he didn't ask for her consent. But I'm sure he had his reasons to do it, he didn't have the madness in him. I have seen that first hand with…" She stopped what she was saying and shook her head.

"I know the reasons why he did it but that still doesn't make it okay for either of you to blindly accept the fact that her choice was taken from her!"

My father was done with the conversation. He slammed his palms on the table as he stood up. I didn't bother to flinch. His show of dominance didn't frighten me. It hadn't since I was a child. I rose from my chair and stared right back at him. "You will respect your Alpha. What he says is law. Don't forget where he will sit in a few years. Our pack won't be the only one he dictates."

I snarled as my wolf fought to get to the surface. She wasn't going to let him talk to me this way. The magical strands around us intensified. "You have questioned his rule for years but now that you find out that he has a mate, everything has changed?"

My mother planted a hand on my father's chest and shook her head. "A man calms down when he finds the one. He isn't so reckless. When an Alpha finds his mate, it means he is ready to lead. Why do you think she was taken from him? Someone doesn't want him taking his rightful place with Pack Law."

I closed my eyes and took a step back, my food was still untouched. "Thanks for dinner, Mom." I didn't usually back down from a challenge but I knew this wasn't the kind of challenge that any of us were prepared for. I could have stayed with my parents but what good would that have done? I had been staying at the Crimson Manor since everything had happened with Jade. I closed the door behind me and was surprised when no one followed me out. They knew how I felt and that was all that mattered. Maybe one day my dad would stop living with such archaic thoughts. My eyes roved the wooded property behind my parent's home. Maybe it was time I started to build my own.

I shook my head. Maybe not. Maybe when we got Jade back, I would just live with her. That would be better than hopping back and forth. We were both the black sheep out of all of this. I hoped she still wanted something to do with me when she got back.

I pulled my phone out of my pocket and scrolled through the contact list. My finger hovered over the one person I hadn't spoken to in ages. The one person I wished would just come home. I clicked the name and listened as it went immediately to voicemail. My heart felt like it was ripped out of my chest.

*"It's Lucas, sorry I couldn't get to the phone right now, leave a message."*

Just hearing his voice did something to my insides. It made me not feel as angry at our parents anymore but it didn't make me feel less sad. I grasped onto the nearest tree for support as my legs buckled beneath me. I gritted my teeth till it was painful but still the tears spilled from my eyes.

Would I ever get better? Would the pain ever stop?

## CHAPTER 29
JADE

I mulled over the information that Damian had bestowed upon me as I walked back to my shared room. But the closer I got to that room, I knew I couldn't go there. I took a detour and ended up in a common area where people were sparring and playing board games. Everyone ignored me as I walked through, observing. Everyone but Bee, her eyes met mine and an emotion I couldn't place passed over her face. She waved me over.

I sat down beside her at the small, square, wooden table. She had a tablet in front of her and was looking at pictures of a little girl. "This is my daughter."

"She's beautiful," She was blonde like her mother but instead of sharing the same bright blue eyes like Bee had, she had brown eyes. They reminded me of Lucas. I pushed the thought down.

"Damian has her, like he has all of our children. Either that or we have nowhere else to go."

I frowned. "What do you mean?"

"Damian kidnapped our children from school or on playdates. He had everything perfectly calculated and if he couldn't take something important to us, he changed us. I was lucky to not have a wolf forced on me but the rest in here? Most of them are wolves and witches or humans that are now wolves like you."

My heart hurt. This was so much bigger than I had imagined. Of course he had created an army. The humans that had been forced to turn had nowhere else to go. They didn't know about pack dynamic or what life as a wolf was really like. All they had was this place. I remembered how lost I had felt after I had been turned and I had people that were looking out for me. But the witches that were also wolves? Where did they belong in this? Then the ones that had their family members taken? I pinched the bridge of my nose to keep the burning from behind my eyes. I couldn't afford to cry. I had kept myself from crying this entire day and now my eyes were betraying me.

"Sheeva also has a niece that's here, but she hasn't been permitted to see her. Damian lets me see my daughter on occasion."

"Where is he keeping them?"

I was surprised that she had an answer for me. "He keeps them in a building similar to this. I think it was an abandoned boarding school. They have nice rooms and get an education. They have no idea what is really happening to them there but we know."

The sadness in this room was thick. "What can you do about that?"

Bee leaned back and sighed hard. "Nothing. We are prisoners here and the ones that aren't prisoners? They have powerful magic and they are very happy to kneel at Damian's feet."

"Why would they do that?"

Bee shrugged. "There are many reasons. The witches feel like they've been at the bottom of the food chain for too long. The Vampires are tired of being afraid of the werewolves and their poisonous bite." At my look of surprise she chuckles. "Oh yes, your bite will kill a witch and a vampire. Possibly more than just that. How do you think the wolves are at the top of the food chain?"

"Then how is it possible that a witch can be

turned into a werewolf?" I didn't know if it was safe to ask these questions but my mind was spinning with all the new information. I needed more. I needed to know it all that way I could put together a plan. I knew Rafe was plotting but I couldn't rely on him. What if he got bored with all of this and decided I wasn't worth it anymore? The last thing I wanted to be was a sitting duck.

Bee shook her head. "I wish I knew. You'll have to ask Damian." Her eyes flashed angrily. "I heard you're getting rather cozy with him."

I couldn't blow my cover, even if it meant the people here would hate me. "I want revenge."

"On Rafe Crimson?" She raised her light brows. "That's funny considering what I saw in your head."

I smiled. "You can read thoughts?"

"When I was in control of your body, I saw things. I know what he did to you but I also know you're confused by it all and you want to know why. You know he isn't a psychopath that did it like Damian is doing."

I leaned forward and my voice dropped low. "There are things I need to do while I'm here. I had my chance to run and leave you all behind. Remember that when I need something from you."

There was no point in denying what she saw in my head. If she wanted to use that against me, then so be it. But I wasn't going to let her think I was a traitor.

A voice spoke in my mind as I walked out of the room. *"We will rally behind the one that saves our children, then we will die to destroy the man that did this to us. If you have a plan, we will ready ourselves."*

I hadn't done anything to deserve their loyalty but I had stayed and I guess that was enough. I doubted they had many that would care about them. I didn't know them but I knew I had to do something. There were too many innocents involved. But first, I had to talk to Lucas and I was dreading that conversation more than anything else.

Lucas was waiting for me on my bed this time. He wasn't wearing a shirt and his bronzed body had started to put on weight again. He didn't look so emaciated anymore. His eyes met mine and I was shocked by how handsome he was. But as I continued to stare at him I wanted to beat myself up for not seeing it sooner. He looked just like Tracey except he favored his father more.

"What did Damian want?" He lounged back on

my pillows and for a moment I wondered if he was trying to seduce me. The corner of his mouth picked up and I knew instantly that was what he was trying to do. There had been nothing remotely sexual between us but this was different. His body language had warning bells going off in my head.

"He had lots of information he wanted to share with me." I sat on the edge of his bed and put my face in my hands. Before I knew it he was up and out of my bed. He wrapped his arms around my shoulders and I relaxed into him. My body seemed to sigh with relief but Nalia growled in my mind. She didn't like this one bit. I shooed her away mentally. It felt good to have human contact again. To be touched. When was the last time someone had touched me? Hugged me? I wrapped my arms around his bare waist and held on like it was a lifeline.

He knelt down in front of me and cupped my face between his hands. "If you don't want to be touched, say the word. I know you haven't had the opportunity to consent to so much in your life recently."

"What's going on, Lucas?" He had never been this touchy with me before. He had always kept his distance.

"I didn't realize how much I cared about you till they took you away from here. You have been the one thing they have given me in five years that has meant something. I don't know if it's because they are going to use you against me or if it's something else but I don't want to take you for granted. I want you to know that I care. That I am your ally."

I brushed a curl from his forehead and my face fell. "Thank you for being my friend. Your presence has made this so much easier on me but I have a question for you." I didn't know if I wanted to ask him about Tracey or not, so I blurted out the first thing that came to mind. "Aren't you gay?"

He planted his hands on either of my shoulders and his body shook with laughter. "I'm bi, actually."

I didn't know if it was relief that made my shoulders relax or something else. I laughed with him and rolled my eyes. "So you're trying to seduce me right now?"

His face went serious. "If Damian has touched you in ways that you don't want to speak of, I will wipe your mind clean of the encounter with my own hands. I will do what it takes for you to feel whole again. If he forces himself on you and you need to feel in control, I will be here to let you have control back."

I launched myself off of the bed and wrapped my arms around his neck. I didn't know if I went through trauma that I would want him to have to be my healing balm but the thought and care that went into those words were enough to be a balm over my soul. "He hasn't touched me or tried anything like that but thank you for being open with me and trying. That means more to me than anything else."

I could feel his body relax against mine. "Is that the only question you had to ask me?"

It was now or never. "Is Tracey your sister?"

His face fell then. "That night they threw you in here, I wondered if it was my mind playing tricks on me that you smelled like her. Now I know they had done that intentionally to hurt me."

I rubbed my hands up and down his bare arms. "I didn't know. I promise you I didn't until Damian told me today."

"You saw her, didn't you? Before you came back a different person and willing to work with the devil?"

"Do you want me to tell you about her?" I was treading carefully. As carefully as I could manage.

"Please," He sat on my bed and stared at me like an anxious puppy.

"She has magic like you," I swallowed hard. "Damian admitted that you still have magic inside of you somewhere."

Lucas pulled his bottom lip into his mouth and nodded. "Yes, I know I have magic still. That's why Micah brought me the tarot deck. I was always better as a Seer. Other magic wasn't easy for me. My granny is an earth witch. She gets her magic from the plants and the sun. She's a green witch." He chuckled. "But she could never help me with my magic because it dealt with bones, stones, and cards. My magic is different. I don't know how or why but I can't see the tethers to the world around me like other witches can."

"Wait, that's a thing?"

He grinned. "Yes, magic is a complex thing. It lives and breathes in the air around us. I learned so much when I left the Crimson Pack, but life outside of the Pack Land was both easier and harder. Being bi in the witch community is openly accepted, whereas being bi in the wolf community is frowned upon. The wolves aren't nearly as progressive as the witches. I hate to say it. Wolves mate for life and unfortunately, there has never been a same-sex mate pairing. At least not any that the packs are aware of."

"And witches?" I prompted.

"Witches celebrate life and love. Magic can be created in love and lust. Depending on the type of witch, she could be more powerful if she takes on more lovers." He shrugged. "I wouldn't know though. I have never experienced that. I fell in love with Damian and this is where that got me. I think my judgment is messed up."

I shook my head. "Looks and actions can be deceiving. I have been tricked many times. Rafe Crimson not being the first."

His eyebrows pulled together. "Rafe Crimson? He's about as good as they come, Jade."

I laughed and rolled my eyes. "I heard he was your protector but unfortunately, I didn't get to experience that side of him."

Lucas narrowed his eyes at me. "Rafe was always kind to everyone but he never took anyone's shit. Something must have happened in the last five years."

I chewed on the inside of my lip. "I heard he killed his father."

Lucas's face crumbled. "That will do it. Do you know why?"

I shook my head. "No, but I adore his mother. She got me a job before all of this," I waved my hands around dramatically. "happened."

"Alice was always the den mom to all of us. She never judged me when everyone else did. I would imagine that's where Rafe got his kindness from."

"Rafe is the one that forced the wolf on me." I could no longer hold the words back. The man that Lucas had known was gone. At least that was what I told myself, even if Nalia didn't believe it.

Lucas watched me carefully before he cocked his head to the side. "What were you doing when he changed you?"

I bit the inside of my cheek again. It was really starting to feel raw inside of my mouth. "I was at a party but that has nothing to do with this."

He smirked and his entire face changed. It reminded me of Rafe for a moment. "I can see it now, the innocent girl going to the party expecting nothing to happen to her."

I frowned. "That wasn't how it was at all."

"No? So you expected the bad boys to not prey on you? You smell innocent. You smell good. You have ever since they threw you in here and you expected no one to harm you?"

I blinked. "That's not it…"

"Then tell me how it is,"

And as he sat there across from me, I realized something that I hadn't thought of before. "I was very naive I suppose."

The smirk fell from his face. "Aren't we all, love? At one point we trust too easily and that's how we get hurt." He sighed and leaned back. "That just doesn't sound like Rafe, okay?"

Lucas wasn't the first one that had said that. I had heard it around the pack, I had seen the look on his mother's face. I had even talked to his little brother.

All I could manage was a nod. Who was the real Rafe? What was I missing? Up until I had been taken, I had seen little bits but not enough to actually know *who* he was behind the snark and dark looks.

## CHAPTER 30
RAFE

I grabbed the ends of my hair and pulled gently. It had been a while since I had a haircut but I couldn't take the time to do anything mundane like that when I needed to figure out how I was going to help Jade. I had no doubts that she could get herself out but I wanted to help. I needed to help. My wolf would have it no other way. I had to at least try to help for his sake.

But we were practically sitting ducks. No matter how many times we had looked at the situation, there didn't seem to be a solution unless we didn't care what happened to the other families involved. There was also the possibility that the witches were lying to her to get her to stop fighting.

Archer leaned back in the leather recliner across

the war room. "We could always say to hell with the other people and just rescue your mate. No one would know if he punished those people. We wouldn't know."

He had said exactly what I was thinking. Mav wrinkled his nose. "I don't like that idea. Jade would never forgive us. She stayed back for a reason."

Knox held up his beer in salute. "Jade is already a hellhound, the last thing we need is to piss her off further."

I sighed as my eyes turned to Tracey, she was sharpening a knife and was the farthest from the Guardians, I didn't blame her. They were starting to annoy me too.

Gabriel leaned across the bar on the far side of the room. "We need a distraction."

I looked over at one of the quietest Guardians. "I'm listening."

"A distraction to get inside, I don't know, to look through the maps. To survey the room."

An idea popped into my head. "We have to somehow get in there."

Archer grinned as he shot up from the recliner. "I volunteer as tribute."

"You've never even read those books," Tracey grumbled.

Archer made a face. "I've seen the movies."

"Not the same thing," she sighed.

"Totally the same thing," he retorted.

I rubbed my temples. "What did I tell you all about being in here? This is a place to talk strategy. We can't afford to be so flippant about this.

Mav cracked his neck. "Gabriel is right, we have to be ready to either send someone inside and cause a distraction or get a message to Jade."

"But that still doesn't solve the problem of families in danger," Tracey rolled her shoulders. "We should have brought snacks."

My eyes went to the refrigerator behind the bar. Mav shook his head. "It's empty."

"We have been at this for hours." I ran my hand down my face. "Maybe we will have fresh ideas tomorrow, especially with full stomachs."

Archer and Knox practically raced each other out of the war room. Tracey gritted her teeth together. "Children."

I couldn't keep the laugh from bubbling out of my mouth. I shook my head. "Go get some rest and food. Your dad will have my head if you don't start eating again. You were always the first one in line at dinner, now you hardly show up."

Tracey didn't look at me as she passed. "Why isn't he here?"

I didn't know if it was my place to tell her what her dad planned. "I think he was busy. We have been communicating a lot better lately, so he isn't here because of us not getting along."

She nodded like she knew.

Gabriel was the last out the door. "Have you been to your home recently?"

I was about to say something about the Manor when I realized that wasn't what he was talking about. All I could do was shake my head.

"You should go there, you'll want to have your own place when she comes back. Your wolf will push you to have a den ready for her and your future pups."

My mother had warned me of that when I told her Jade was my mate. She had told me that I would have a drive to keep my mate safe and have a place for her. I had a home but I hadn't done much with it. I had stayed at the main house but now I realized he was right.

"If you need any help with the house or getting it ready, let me know."

He was gone after I didn't say anything. What could I say? How could I go there now? She wasn't here and there was still a chance that we wouldn't get her back. And if that happened? I would die anyway. Even though we hadn't completed the bond, I knew what my fate would be.

When I had taken my father's place as Alpha, my mom and my brother both moved into the main house. It was a sign of respect to me. It would be my home now. My mother had no problem giving it up. I couldn't imagine the pain she experienced with having to live there without him. Her life mate. She would live an immortal life without him. I couldn't understand or even fathom what that felt like and I never would. Female wolves would live on without their mates, but males couldn't. I didn't understand it but it was the way it had always been. Females were needed to raise pups. The females were essential to keeping the pack moving and operating as normal, even if something happened to the Alpha. Which was exactly what my mother had done. She had kept the pack going and without worry while I adjusted into my place. She had always been there for every single member of the pack and I had been nothing but rude to her over and over. I owed her so much.

I locked up the war room and looked at the well-worn path in the dirt. Some grass had sprouted up in places but for the most part, it was clear. I took a deep breath as I turned down the path to my parent's home- my home. All of my best and worst memories were here. It was the place I had first transformed, the place I had learned to ride a bike. The home was so full of love that I knew it would choke me as soon as I saw it again.

Most of the grass had grown up around the white farm-style house in the middle of the cleared acre. If I wasn't careful, I would have to get a tractor out here. I shoved my hands deep into my pockets and maneuvered around the stickers and weeds before I saw my brother sitting on the front steps.

"What are you doing here?" My voice came out in a whisper like I would wake spirits if I spoke any louder. Like this place held demons instead of happiness.

Ford blinked up at me and flipped his ball cap around. "I was just visiting. I needed some quiet. Laura had her twins up at the main house and the crying hasn't stopped."

A smile touched my lips and I sat on the steps beside him. "I'm sure the babies aren't the only loud mouths around there." I could just picture my mother barking orders at everyone to make sure

Laura was as comfortable as can be. The last baby born at the Manor was four years old now. It would be nice to have new pups to teach.

Ford sighed and it ripped through my chest. "I was thinking about Dad."

I scrunched my nose as emotions flooded me. I didn't know what to say. We didn't talk about him with Mom. If you mentioned him in her presence, the pain that would flash across her face was enough to bring you to your knees. "Yeah?"

Ford smirked. "You don't have to try to comfort me, I know he was sick."

I didn't want to tell him that I knew it was more than that. An investigation hadn't been opened to respect my mother. But I remembered his black, cursed blood like it was yesterday. I had no doubt that I would remember it until the day I died.

I leaned my elbows down onto my knees and shook my head. "I don't know what to say to you. But yeah, he was sick."

"I miss his laugh."

He did have an infectious laugh. It rumbled through him like his wolf was amused too. He had such a good connection with his inner animal, I was sure that was the case. "Yeah, I miss it too."

"You remind me of him," He looked away as he

spoke, like he was too afraid to share his emotions with me. I leaned over and wrapped my arm around his shoulders. They shook gently. How long had he been coming out here to get away from the pack noise? Is this why Gabriel said something? He had been assigned this area to patrol lately.

"I will never be as good as Dad was." It was true. He was the best Alpha we had ever had until the end. He was also the best father. Taking his life had been the hardest thing I had ever had to do besides fight my wolf on turning Jade. That still left a bad taste in my mouth, even if my wolf was content with it. He would have claimed her too, if I hadn't stopped him.

"You'll get there," When Ford looked up at me, his eyes were shining with unshed tears. "Wanna look inside?" He hooked a thumb over his shoulder toward the front door.

I nodded my head. If there was anyone I wanted to help me making this shell a home, it was him.

## CHAPTER 31
JADE

As each day passed, I found myself getting closer to the witches. They were prisoners just as much as I was. It was the wolves that I stayed away from. They were cunning and ruthless. Damian had chosen the right humans to change for his army. They were the bad boys I would have flocked to before. But now I didn't feel that way. I had enough of the bad boys and the trouble. I sat with Sheeva one day when a smaller witch with a limp came barreling into the room. Her mascara was smeared in rivulets down her cheeks and her eyes were wide with panic. Sheeva stood up and grabbed her by the shoulders as I watched a group of wolves follow her in.

I bared my teeth at them as they circled us. "What's going on here?"

"She has something we want," the man at the front of the pack said.

I crossed my arms over my chest. "Which is?"

"Her blood," he shot me a bloodthirsty smile and everything inside of me turned feral. Nalia rose to the surface as a growl rumbled through my chest. The man's smile faltered for a second. "Give her to us and you won't have a problem."

I looked behind me at the small girl and I saw red. Her neck was bleeding like they had tried to bite her, and her arms were clawed up. Her scent told me she wasn't a wolf, but a witch. Something protective rose up inside of me as I turned back to the bloodthirsty wolves. My lips peeled away from my teeth. Who did these bullies think they were?

The tips of my fingers ached as my claws burst through the skin there. I flexed my hands as I prepared for the fight and as the other witches and wolves in the room took a collective step back, I knew I was alone. Which was fine, I wasn't going to let these wolves get away with this, especially when almost everyone knew who I was. These were the exceptions I assumed.

I rolled my neck and shoulders as I smiled. "Well, if you want her, come get her."

I didn't know where the fight inside of me had come from but I had a feeling it had to do with Nalia. They look a look at my eyes and sniffed the air. I had no idea what they had found as their faces paled, but I didn't care. The first one rushed me and I stuck my hand out in defense. The memory of Knox ripping a heart out was still fresh in my mind. Nalia *loved* it. She practically purred as I went over the strategy in my head. Before I could change my mind, I swiped my hand up into his chest cavity. The sound of bones crunching filled the room, but I didn't stop there. I wrapped my fingers around the organ and yanked with all of my strength. The man crumbled at my feet and I threw the heart down beside him even though Nalia was very disappointed that we didn't take a bite out of it. I knew it would show the others I was more dominant, but I wasn't entirely worried about that. There were still two bullies coming at me. Dominance would come later, that is, if I decided to care about it.

I grabbed the other one by the neck and lifted him into the air before my claws pierced his skin and punctured his jugular. I threw him to the ground and went for the next one but he was already gone. He had tucked tail and disappeared.

"Anyone else?" My voice came out in a growl. "These witches are here to help Damian's cause, *our cause*. If anyone of you harms them again, your death will be slow like this one." I kicked the man choking on his own blood.

*Our cause?* I asked Nalia in my head. I hadn't realized she had taken over until now. Until I felt sick at all the bloodshed. My claws sunk back into my fingers and I tried to wipe the ichor on my jeans. It was caked under my nails. I tucked my fingers into fists and jutted my chin into the sky. The only way out of this was with dignity.

*Damian has to trust us. He will be watching that scene over the cameras. We had to make it believable.* Nalia said proudly.

🐾

Damian was lounging on my bed when I came out of the bathroom. Lucas was on his bed, pretending to look at his tarot cards but I knew better. He was hyper-aware of his past love not even ten feet away from him.

"There she is," Damian purred.

I pulled the towel off of my head and tossed it into the hamper. "What do you want?"

"*Our* cause remember?" He smiled at Lucas, who now found the ceiling to be rather interesting, rather than the man staring at him.

I crossed my arms over my chest. I had scrubbed my body until it was raw and I hoped he couldn't smell the weakness. I hoped he couldn't feel it in the air. I had vomited until I felt like I was going to blackout and now I had to pretend like I was okay, like I was going to be all right. "Yes, I remember. I told you that I was on your side, didn't I?"

He narrowed his eyes and nodded. "Yes, but you have given yourself over to the witches here. You have alienated yourself from the wolves."

"Aren't you a witch?"

He regarded me thoughtfully. "Yes, but I thought for sure you would ally with the wolves."

I shrugged one shoulder up. "What can I say? I'm not very predictable."

He hummed. "I suppose. I'm still trying to figure you out, little wolf."

"I thought that was what you wanted. I didn't think you would want me to side with the wolves. You have had me surrounded by them, except my guard and Lucas. But he's still technically a witch, isn't he?" I could feel Lucas's eyes burning into the side of my face.

Damian smirked. "Yes, I suppose you're correct. I guess I should have kept you close to the wolves then?"

"I still can't guarantee that I would befriend them. They are all rogues here. They have their own pack dynamic that I don't care to know. I don't care about their ranks or their dominance or lack thereof."

Damian sat up and a curious look passed over his face. "You like to run alone."

"I have been alone since I was a child, what's new? Pack life doesn't interest me." Pack life only interested me if it had to do with the Crimson Pack and that was it. I still didn't know where I fit in there, but I liked how easy it felt. I liked how good everyone was. Except Rafe, he was still complicated and not exactly good either.

"I like you, Jade Rivers," he muttered as he walked to the door. "Don't make me regret that."

**CHAPTER 32**
JADE

Damian's trust in me meant lots of gifts and the best food that could be made in the cafeteria. I had expected the witches to stay away from me but they embraced me when I finally had the courage to go to them. The wolves had stopped in their tracks and *literally* bowed down to me when I passed them in the halls or the commons. My throat felt thick with emotion as a massive cookie was placed beside my steak for dinner. The serving lady, that I finally recognized as the one that had brought the cake to my room, gave me a tearful smile.

"My daughter was the one you saved the other day," Her voice trembled as she whispered. I bowed my head in response. I didn't know what to say but I knew the witches felt like they owed me. I didn't mind either. It would help me, in the long run, to get out of here.

Lucas was already seated waiting for me. His steak looked pitiful. I switched our trays and took the little one. I wasn't feeling like myself. Usually, I was ravenous but today, I still felt sick about killing those wolves. I wanted to eat, I really did but every time I looked at the meat, all I saw was their blood on my hands. Instead of eating the steak, I took the cookie and broke it into little pieces.

"You know he's watching you, right?" Lucas nodded to my untouched steak.

"I'm aware, I think I'm sick or something."

Lucas scoffed. "Werewolves don't get sick, silly."

I frowned. "We don't?"

"You shouldn't..." He trailed off. "Unless you're getting sick from being kept from your mate."

I rolled my eyes. "Everyone keeps bringing up my mate, but wouldn't I know it if I had one?"

Lucas shrugged. "I've never had a mate, I wouldn't know."

My shoulders fell. "Why does everything have to be so confusing?"

Lucas chuckled. "That's life, baby doll."

I wrinkled my nose at the nickname. He had been trying different ones out since we had our heart to heart. I wasn't really fond of any of them, but he wasn't going to stop until something stuck. "I am not a doll."

He grumbled. "You're right, you're not fragile at all."

I sat up straight as a thought came to me. I leaned forward and brushed his hair away from his face in a flirty manner and whispered, "I think I have a plan."

He raised his brows and leaned closer before he pressed a kiss to the corner of my mouth. "This is dangerous. He's watching you."

"We need a distraction,"

"Kissing in the middle of the cafeteria will do that." He smirked as he leaned in closer and licked up the side of my neck. I shivered and felt all the eyes in the room turn to us.

"We need something more dangerous." I panted.

He leaned back in his seat but I stayed poised above the table, like I was waiting for more.

"Yes, I agree but the timing isn't right."

I pouted. The only place that there wasn't surveillance was the bathroom. We had never ventured in there together but this was different. Things were getting more dangerous. Even though the wolves bowed down to me, I could taste their anger. I had taken valuable members of their pack. They would retaliate. I had to be ready. I had to get the witches out of here safely.

My hands shook as I turned the shower on. Lucas peeled his shirt off as he walked into the room and then closed the bathroom door behind him. "We won't have much time."

I nodded. "Can you find the witches' families?"

He shook his head. "I told you that my magic doesn't work like that. We would need blood from one of the families in order to track the children. I don't deal in blood magic."

I sighed. "But someone can?"

He pressed his lips together. "My granny can."

"But how are we going to be able to get her some blood?" I paced across the tile.

"We get one of the witches out," He chewed on his bottom lip. "That's the only way."

I shook my head. "That's too dangerous."

"You're the one that said all of this would be dangerous." He shook his head. "You think *this* is dangerous? Our lives were in danger the moment he brought us here. We will be lucky if we make it out alive, you have to understand that. We might die."

A nervous laugh escaped my lips. "We will *not* die. I won't let us. I won't let you die."

He shook his head like he had already accepted his impending doom. "Then we will talk with Sheeva, but not right away. She will work with us and the cook. We are going to have to make a massive distraction that might kill someone, do you understand?"

"They have to know the risks before we involve them," I pulled my shirt over my head then shimmied my jeans off. We couldn't come out of this bathroom without the evidence that we indeed showered together. They would be watching. He averted his eyes while I stepped under the spray and scrubbed my hair.

"I can promise you, they know the risks and they are completely okay with them."

"And you know your granny will for sure help?" I closed my eyes as the soap ran down my face and near my mouth. I tiled my head back to rinse the shampoo out before I lathered up my hands in conditioner. At least they had given me the good stuff. My blonde hair wasn't dying in here.

"Yes, I promise you that she will be willing to do whatever it takes to get you out."

My eyes snapped open as his words dawned on me. There was still soap on my eyelids. I blinked as the burning set in and tears leaked from my eyes. "You're getting out of here too."

Lucas shook his head. He sat hunched over on the toilet seat and wouldn't look at me. I was somewhat relieved over that but I couldn't get a feel for his emotions without seeing his face. All the steam in the bathroom didn't make it easy to smell his emotions either. I ran my hands over my eyes. Lucas finally whispered, "We will not tell them I am here, do you understand me?"

I kept the water running as I grabbed a towel off of the rack beside the shower door and ran it over my face before I stepped out into the cold air. "Why? Why can't they know you're here?"

Lucas looked up as I was wrapping the towel around my torso. "They already lost me once. If something happens while we are fighting to get out of here, then I don't want them to go through the emotions of having to lose me again or knowing they could have had me. I don't want them to go through the 'what ifs'. You let me die and you leave me dead if something happens. You don't let them wonder or harbor pain over me." The emotions waging war on his face were enough for me to promise him that I wouldn't say anything. He showered quickly while I stewed over what he said.

When he got out of the shower and wrapped the towel around his waist, he smiled. "No more bad thoughts like death, okay?"

All I could manage was a nod and a fake smile. We had to play the part coming out of the bathroom together. Surprisingly enough Damian wasn't waiting for us like I thought he would be. Micah was lounging on my bed this time.

"We have five minutes to talk before the cameras click back on."

Lucas snorted out a laugh. "What the f-"

"What are you planning?" I interrupted Lucas and stared daggers down at Micah. Lucas and I both still had towels wrapped around us.

"I know you are planning something and I want in. No matter what it is. I am one of the only ones that can get in and out of this place without suspicion." He shrugged like *duh*.

"We need to get one of the witches out."

Micah pressed his lips together. "The only way that's going to happen is if one of them dies."

I shrugged. "So be it. Magic is a powerful thing."

Micah bit his lip. "No, you don't understand. Damian's power far surpasses any other witch I have ever encountered. Now that you have allied yourself with the witches, he will be looking for you to try something with them."

I shook my head. "Then we cannot plan this. We can't go forward. I won't sacrifice anyone for my cause. We will have to think of something else."

## CHAPTER 33
JADE

I was still trying to think of a plan when Damian slid into the seat across from me in the common room. Everyone went eerily quiet as he grinned at me and the obvious fear in the room.

"Good morning, Damian," I said casually like I hadn't been plotting his demise for the last few hours.

"Good morning, Jade, you seem to be in a good mood today." He watched as the witches and wolves quickly filed out. The room had been lively and full of energy just a few minutes prior. He sucked the life out of it all.

"Making enemies and killing people will do that to you," I grinned like I wasn't bothered with what was haunting my sleep.

"And possibly some good sex?" He leaned forward on his elbows and smiled smugly.

I crossed my arms over my chest. "I'm not sure I know what you mean."

"I didn't have the privilege of sleeping with Lucas, but I have heard rumors he's a very selfless lover."

Blood rushed to my cheeks and as much as I wanted to pretend to be embarrassed I couldn't be. It was all real. "You came here to talk about my sex life?"

He titled his head from side to side. "I find it interesting that you can stomach doing such a thing when you have a mate."

I rolled my eyes. "I don't know why you concern yourself with it. Maybe I'm polyamorous."

"That would be fine, if you weren't a wolf. They mate for life."

I clenched my jaw. "I never agreed to any mating, so not yet I'm not."

He chuckled. "Once you discover that mating bond, it'll be painful to be with others."

I leaned across the space between us. "Why are you so obsessed with me?"

He bopped me on the nose. "Oh little wolf, I'm not obsessed with *you*. I'm obsessed with what you can give me." His eyes twinkled with mischief as he stood up to walk away.

I looked up at him unimpressed. "And what if I'm obsessed with what you can give me?"

He grinned. "Then I think we have the perfect partnership, my pet."

I could feel Nalia rising up to his challenge inside of me. I had to think soothing thoughts to get her calm. The last thing we needed was to start a fight with the man that could kill thousands with one word. Based on how many witches he had here under his thumb, there were thousands of kids that would be collateral damage if I wasn't careful.

Except it didn't matter if I was careful that night. Plans had been made without me, at least I became aware of that when we were eating dinner and Lucas refused to talk to me. No matter what I said or did, he just continued to eat his food like he couldn't hear me.

I rolled my eyes at his dramatics. "You can call me baby doll if you'd like or any of the other ridiculous nicknames you came up with."

Lucas smirked. "That's your secret weapon to get me to talk?"

I raised my brows. "It worked, though."

He sighed before he took a massive bite out of his hamburger. I could feel it in the air that something wasn't right. It was like my wolf senses were tingling. I couldn't put my finger on it.

"Lucas, what's going on?"

Based on the way his eyes crinkled, he was about to lie to me. But before he could get the chance an explosion rocked the building. I watched in slow-motion as I was thrown from the table I sat at and Lucas was pinned beneath it. My head connected with the wall and a high pitch noise filled my ears. Dust fell from the…

I blinked. There was no ceiling above me, all that was there was was black sky above us. I tried to sit up but my body wouldn't listen to my internal commands.

*Nalia?* I thought to my other half, but she was silent. Finally, after a few more attempts I was able to rise from the rubble around me. Everything hurt and none of my senses were functioning properly. All I could hear were muffled screams and that high pitch noise. I coughed into my elbow as I tried to get to Lucas but there was too much happening around me.

A massive piece of ceiling fell from the sky and I

watched as it came down to crash into me. Except it didn't. It was suspended in the air above my head.

"Jade!" My senses came back to me all at once and I stumbled forward over more debris. What happened?

"Jade!" This time I could hear my name being called clearly. I choked on my breath again as I stumbled toward the voice. Was it Lucas calling me or Damian? I couldn't differentiate with my hearing still coming back to me.

I knew it had to be Damian calling me as soon as I noticed Lucas laying on the ground unconscious under the pieces of picnic tables we had been sitting at. Blood rolled down his forehead and his eyes fluttered briefly before he went still again. Nothing else mattered as I fought my way through the throng of people trying to get away from the fire on the other side of the room. Someone was screaming as I fought my way across the rubble but I didn't allow myself to get distracted. I fell into the dust and sheetrock beside my sweet friend.

"Lucas!" I tried to pull the table pieces off of him but my werewolf strength was gone.

"Let me help you," a gentle voice said beside me.

I fell back away from Lucas's still body and felt

my insides crumble like the building. Tears fell from my face as I realized that Lucas could die from this. This was what I had been trying to prevent. He had predicted his own death but I couldn't let that happen. I wouldn't let that happen.

Damian lifted the jagged pieces of the table with his magic, I assumed as they floated above his body without a tether or evidence otherwise. They crashed somewhere in the distance as I pulled Lucas into my arms and brushed his hair from his face. Damian leaned over to check for a pulse while I rocked back and forth.

Damian sat back on his heels. "He's still alive. His pulse is strong. His wolf won't be able to heal him though. Someone blew up the wolfsbane closet."

It hit me like a ton of bricks. This was the distraction. This was what I had been left out of. I pulled Lucas from the rubble and into my arms. I stumbled over bodies and more pieces of the room before I got him to one of the hallways. I looked back at the damage to the cafeteria but the dust was still thick in the air and now smoke was starting to join it. Damian was nowhere to be seen and neither was Micah. I looked down at my friend and wondered if he would be safe here. I couldn't sit out on the rescue efforts. The building was on fire and there was no telling how many people would die if I didn't go in there to help.

I pressed a quick kiss to Lucas's hairline before I jumped back into the madness. Damian was using his magic to lift pieces of wood and sheetrock from the victims. I was no use on that front but where the fire was, I knew I could help. I rushed through the wall that was on fire and right into the kitchen. I immediately spotted Micah. He held a syringe up before he put it in his pocket. Laying on the ground at his feet was Bee. Her head was at an odd angle and her limbs were sprawled out around her. I immediately sprang to action. She could be saved, right?

Micah grabbed me around my middle and stopped me from going down to her. Stopped me from feeling that she was already gone. I didn't realize I was crying until a sob erupted from my lips. She was my friend. She had a daughter. A family. She was more than this place. She was more than this death. I fought his hold and fell to my knees beside her. I hardly knew her but she had been my friend. She didn't deserve this. Her family didn't deserve this. My hands fluttered over her peaceful face as another sob wracked through my body.

Micah pulled me into his arms and I felt myself break again. My entire body shuddered with it. Where was Nalia? She was the only one that could help me.

"We have a few minutes before Damian comes this way. The fire is superficial and can be put out easily. You can fall apart but know that she sacrificed herself for this cause. She sacrificed herself for her daughter." Micah whispered into my hair. I would avenge her. I would avenge them all. I nodded my head against his shoulder and fell back to my knees beside her. "You have to get up, Jade. She was a traitor. She deserved this death."

"No," I whispered. I knew the moment Damian walked through the flames. It was like the air had been sucked from the room. "No!"

I fell forward and brushed her blonde hair from her face. The sobs only increased.

"You heard him, Jade," Damian commanded. "She was a traitor. There is no use in these theatrics. "I understand your grief but you must let her go. Micah did what he had to do."

My eyes turned up at the man that had guarded my room. Of course he was the one that had killed her. He would do it quickly so she felt no pain. She had sacrificed herself. I nodded once before I tried to wipe the tears from my face. "Will her body be brought to her family?"

"Traitors don't deserve such honors." Before I could reply her body was in flames at my feet. I jumped back in horror and dread. He was burning her body. What were we to do now? How would we get her blood to the pack? Her sacrifice had been for nothing. My face fell. "But Micah will be permitted to go to her family and tell them what he did. He will bring her ashes with him."

Micah smiled gleefully and it caused nausea to fill my stomach. The cook that had befriended me busted through the wall of flames next. When she saw Bee's body burning her face fell too. She understood what we had lost. She didn't allow any tears as she looked down at the witch she had cared for. The witch we had all cared for.

Damian sighed. "This is all very unfortunate." He twirled his fingers and her body stopped burning. He snapped his fingers and then the ashes collected in the air. Damian materialized a long thin glass beaker. The ashes collected into it before he put a cork on the top. He handed the remains of our friend to Micah before he wrapped his arm around me and led me from the room.

His voice echoed around the war zone we walked through. "We will have to find another home."

## CHAPTER 34
RAFE

"You know, arguing about such things is completely pointless," Tracey muttered at the dinner table. Tonight was another full moon and we were preparing to go out again as a pack. But as per usual, Knox and Archer were arguing over anatomy.

Knox snorted. "You're a woman, you wouldn't understand it."

Tracey folded her arms over her chest. "You think I don't understand when a woman's worth is practically decided based on her chest?"

Knox leaned back in his chair. "Don't forget her ass."

Tracey had her spoon halfway to her mouth when he spoke. She looked up with a serious face and threw the entire spoon with rice at his head. The glob of rice hit the center of his forehead and Ford barked out a surprised laugh beside him. In response, Knox wiped off the rice and smeared it across my brother's face. Ford tried to dodge it, but all it did was make a bigger mess across his head.

I leaned back in my chair as the rest of the pack laughed and the new twins garbled from their car seats on the floor. It felt almost normal again. Except there was just one missing piece.

*My mate.*

As if Mav could read my thoughts he leaned over and patted my shoulder. "We will come up with something. Our pack will be whole again."

I nodded my head as I finished off the stewed chicken on my plate. I didn't bother with tasting it. I stood up and filed out of the room. It gave the rest of the pack permission to get up too. My shirt came off first then my jeans before my wolf ripped through my skin. I felt myself sigh with relief as I faded into oblivion and let my wolf take over. I liked to be present most of the time, but not this time. I could feel myself fading like I was taking a nap.

. . .

When I came to, there was blood all over my bare chest and I had zero ideas of where I was. The woods didn't look familiar and there was the roaring of a waterfall nearby. I didn't remember there being a waterfall on our property but it had been a long time since I had been on patrols or even looked at the maps. Patrols had been my excuse to find a willing female to romp with.

I was a shit Alpha. I should have memorized the border of our lands instead of relying on the flag markers set up around the property. I needed to do better. I had to do better.

I pressed my palm into my forehead and laid back down on the leaves. The snow would be here any day now and it would be even harder to get to Jade then. The chill was already heavy in the air. I rolled over onto my stomach and groaned. Thankfully my wolf had disposed of us both beside a body of water. The smell coming off of me was intense. My wolf was practically snoring in my head.

*What did you kill?*

Surprise, surprise, I got zero response.

The water shocked me from my sleepy state as I plunged into it. It was crystal clear and I knew if I had been here before, I would remember it. I swam under the waterfall and came up on the other side in a cave. It was still too deep to stand up so I swam for a moment before I pulled my body up on the ledge and laid back. The cave was hardly big enough to stand up in. The sound of the waterfall slapping the surface of the water was deafening as it echoed off of the walls around me. It was almost too much with my heightened senses.

*Rafe, we have a situation at the manor.* Knox's words blasted through my head and the peaceful moment I was having.

*Can it wait?*

*Definitely not. The wolf that escorted Jade through the woods that night is here. He has witch blood.*

I was out of the water faster than I thought I could move. Nothing else mattered but getting to the pack house and my wolf agreed. Fur rippled across my arms before I shifted again and let my wolf lead me back to the manor.

Not just any wolf could transform multiple times a day. My body was still healing from the transformation the night before but it didn't matter. My wolf didn't care either. I would handle the soreness. All that mattered was getting to my Guardians. We shot across the Pack Lands at a speed I didn't know possible, especially after shifting the night before.

I skidded across the dirt in front of the manor. Knox was standing out front with a pair of boxers and a t-shirt folded neatly between his hands. My mother's mouth was hanging open from the doorway. I had never managed this much power before. I prepared myself mentally for the change back to be brutal. A few pops and cracks later and I was standing in front of my family stark nude. I grabbed the clothes and put them on quickly, expecting soreness and fatigue but I was met with neither.

The man that had the witch blood took a step out of the manor then. His blue eyes were clear as he looked at us all. Then he showed me his neck. "Alpha."

"What can I do for you?" I leaned forward to shake his hand. His grip was steady and firm.

"We have to work fast, but I have brought the blood of a witch that has a daughter being held hostage. As far as I know, all of the children are kept in the same place." He held up a vial full of dark red blood.

"How do I know you're telling the truth?" I didn't know why I asked it. I could smell it in the air that his words were honest.

"Because I care about those children there. Before I was the warden to Jade Rivers, I was the warden at that school. They wiped my memories on how to get there, but I remember the faces. There are many things I have done wrong and..." He paused to swallow. "I want to redeem myself."

I knew all about that feeling so I leaned forward, clapped him on the shoulder, and led him to our witch, Granny.

A world map was laid out on the table when we entered her cottage. Granny shook her head and called Tracey forward before she took the vial from the man named, Micah. "I am not a blood witch, but I have a feeling that Tracey is."

She shook her head as panic flashed across her face. "I am no such thing. I don't know anything about being a witch."

"Witches know how to identify other witches. You will need to say these words," she held a book out to Tracey. "Then spill the contents on the map. We don't have much time. The magic around the vial is already starting to wear off."

Tracey took a deep breath and read the words out loud. "*Vala chosa velum treka brumiam.*" The blood turned black as it was poured on the map. I expected it to stick to the parchment, but instead it slithered across the paper like oil. I pressed my fist to my mouth as the black blood started to circle one area.

Granny looked up at Carden. The pissant was still hanging around. I raked my fingers through my hair and shook my head. This just kept getting better and better. "Get the pack directory in the Manor. We are going to need to know if there is a pack in the middle of Cedar Springs. I'm going to look into my resources and see if there are any covens in the area. We will have to be really careful about this."

Tracey hadn't moved from the spot she was in. Her eyes hadn't left the paper either. Knox and the rest of the Guardians were standing outside. I patted Knox on the shoulder. "Stay with Tracey."

I nodded to Mav. "Meet me at the War Room with your fighting leathers. We are rescuing some kids tonight, boys."

## CHAPTER 35
RAFE

Micah was on my heels from the war room. He was our best asset at the moment. He knew what we were facing when we got there and he knew how to beat the man keeping Jade hostage. I didn't know a man named Damian, though he apparently knew me well. I scratched my head as I went over any possible enemies and the only ones I could think of were the dads of the girls I had thought could be my mate.

I winced. I knew damn well that none of those girls had been my mate but it was the right thing to say at the time when I thought sex was the only thing that mattered in my life.

Micah had filled us in on everything there was to know about him, or rather, everything there was to know that he knew. He was young and handsome but ruthlessly cunning. There were zero last names that Micah could think of. The guy kept to himself for the most part, except when he spoke to Jade. He had taken a liking to her.

Tracey met me at the front of the manor. Her face was grim but she was still wearing her battle leathers. I was afraid for her to go on this mission but I wasn't going to make her stay behind either. "Are you sure you want to go?"

"I've trained beside all of you my entire life. I will not miss this." She grinned but it was anything but friendly.

"Your dad is going to have my head," I muttered darkly.

She shrugged. "He'll get over it."

I doubted that very much.

"This is small potatoes," Micah finally said as all the Guardians stretched. "There won't be as many guards in place but once we break out the kids, they will tighten up security for where Jade is. She will also have less protection."

"She'll know we've gotten the kids out, right?" Knox rolled his shoulders. He preferred fighting in his wolf form but it made it harder to maneuver in small buildings. He was going to be grouchy tonight. He had trained to partial shift, which was going to be his method tonight. I hoped. The last thing I needed-

I stopped my thoughts there. I had zero doubts when it came to the men who swore to protect me. The men who had been by my side since I was a child. I knew that if anyone could do it, it was them. I looked into each of their faces before I nodded.

Micah's face went grim. "No, I doubt she will know. I won't be returning either. As soon as I do, Damian will know that I had something to do with it and he'll punish Jade in front of me as my punishment. It's better that she knows nothing about this operation or my involvement."

"Wait, you didn't fill her in?" Tracey asked as she tucked a knife in her boot. Her claws were lethal enough but if wolfsbane was involved like last time, she would be defenseless.

Micah pinched his lips together. "No, we didn't. We didn't want there to be suspicion in case Damian decided to take his wrath out on her and she couldn't handle the thought of knowing someone would die in order to do this. It was the only way."

Anger flashed through me. I understood why

they kept her in the dark but I didn't like it. "Is she okay?"

Micah nodded. "The explosion was minor and we made sure she was far enough from the blast when it went off. We wouldn't put her in danger. We knew that if something happened to her you wouldn't care about the children."

"That isn't true," Tracey argued.

I held my hand up. "No, it is true. If you had harmed her intentionally, I wouldn't be helping you right now. Your body would be floating downriver."

Micah's face paled. "She's your mate, I don't blame you."

I lifted my chin. "That's why she was targeted, isn't it?"

Micah licked his bottom lip. "Yes."

"This Damian character knows a lot more about you than even we do. We had no idea she was your mate when they kidnapped her." Archer grimaced.

Gabriel rolled his eyes. "Speak for yourself. The signs were all there. You're all dumb."

Knox snorted. "We are not dumb, we just sometimes miss the obvious clues but Mav and I definitely knew."

That explained how they tried to bait me

several times when it came to her. He shrugged like it was no big deal while Mav paled too. "I had my suspicions but I wasn't going to do anything disrespectful. Knox was the one that made all the naughty plans."

I lifted a brow as my eyes rested on my best friend. "Oh?"

Tracey growled. "You are all pig-headed idiots." She clapped her hands together. "Now that we have gotten that out of the way, let's go get these kids then go get our girl. You all talk a lot for men."

We took several different vehicles until we were about five miles from the area they were holding the children. Knox rolled his shoulders before he grinned at me in the dark. "I love a good fight."

I chuckled. "Yes, I know. You pick them with everyone."

Knox shrugged as he got out of the car. "They just can't handle the heat I'm packing."

Tracey grumbled something under her breath as she joined us. Micah had stayed behind and I had only permitted that because Mav had stayed with him. Taking all of the Guardians and the Alpha off of the Pack Lands wasn't smart. They needed to have defenses still. Mav and Granny would protect my people until we returned.

"If that wolf led us to a trap, I'm going to be the first to rip his throat out," Archer whispered.

I ignored all of them. There was no point in getting worked up over how aggravating they were. I had known how they were when they swore to live and die by my side. I just had no idea how much worse it could get.

I blinked and my night vision took over. It was time.

Knox took up the front of our party and Gabriel took up the back. I walked beside Tracey but not because I felt like I needed to protect her. We walked side by side because we worked the best together. When my friends had left for Guardian training, Tracey had stayed behind. Not because she didn't want to be a Guardian, no, she wanted that more than anything. She stayed behind because she was a woman and women weren't permitted to be Guardians. They were too valuable. To give her empowerment back, I asked her to train with me. Every day we had woken up before dawn and trained as wolves and as humans. She fought just as well as the Guardians did. I had seen her challenge them when she thought I wasn't around. I watched as she bested almost every single one of them. The only one she couldn't get down was Knox and he loved to gloat about it.

We lost count of the time it took to get to the building the children were in. As we got closer to the perimeter, Gabriel broke free and went to take out the guards waiting. He was back just as quickly as he had left with just a slight scent of blood on him. He grinned in the dark before he gave me a thumbs up. He was usually the calmest of the group but tonight, he was living for the fight.

Tracey shivered beside me as we continued forward.

Gabriel spoke through my Alpha link. I could mind speak to anyone in the pack in or out of my wolf form. My Guardians could communicate with me and with each other through a special bond. *Six down.*

I communicated with Tracey down the Alpha link and she nodded. She was ready. I could see it in her fluid stance. Knox ran ahead of us and spoke down our bond. *Three more down.*

This was our first mission together since they had returned and I was excited but also nervous. There should have been more guards, magic, something. But so far it was too easy. Was this Damian guy this stupid? He was using these kids as leverage but he wasn't protecting them better than this?

When we made it onto the main grounds and I could see the building in the distance, my heart rate picked up. I didn't usually get nervous. I hardly ever had much to lose, but now? It was all different. My mate was involved.

Shots blasted through the night and my first instinct was to run toward it. Knox ran backward for a second as he grinned at me.

Tracey spoke down our bond. *Show off.*

All I could do was snicker in response. The guns stopped shooting a second later and then Archer was beside me. He tossed one of the guns in the air and Tracey rolled her eyes.

## CHAPTER 36
RAFE

The element of surprise was gone. We had to act quickly or Damian would probably send backup. That was the last thing we needed. Yes, we were technically outnumbered and didn't know the layout of this building at all. But Guardians were the elite of the elite. They were the best fighters and the best trackers. They were some of the most dangerous wolves around unless there were wolves enhanced with magic. At the thought, I looked over at Tracey. She had been grumpier than usual since using magic but it was all so new and I couldn't blame her for that. I would have been just as grumpy. All of our worlds had been turned upside down.

I had been pretty grumpy after I had found out

Jade was my mate. A human. I had only gotten grumpier from there.

The guard at the front of the castle-like building was knocked out cold already, thanks to Archer. The door was unlocked but as soon as it swung open, men in ski masks filed down the stairs while their guns went off. We managed to work around the bullets and the Guardians were practically dancing with glee as they took each man down. This was like child's play. They had trained for far more than this. Tracey didn't even have to lift a finger.

Each man was down and dead. We couldn't risk one of them coming to and contacting Damian, if they hadn't done so already.

I put my hand on Tracey's shoulder. "You're going to have to help with the kids. I don't think they're going to trust the blood-covered idiots."

She swallowed hard and nodded her head. She was great with kids. If anyone could do this, it was her. "We have to hurry."

Up the stairs, we went two at a time until we came across one door. Tracey gritted her teeth together as she swiped her hand over the door. There was something there I couldn't see. The door opened a second later and a little girl around the age of four stumbled out. Her purple hair was piled up on her head and her little fists were raised, ready to fight.

"Which one of you is the witch?" Her courage was inspiring. Her voice didn't shake or waiver either.

Tracey took a step forward. "Hello, little one, one of your mothers sent us. We are here to get you out."

"Which mother?" A few little children popped out behind the one with purple hair.

"Her name is Sheeva," Tracey's voice was calm and collected. It also helped that she wasn't covered in blood and gore like the men below.

The little girl lowered her hands. "That's my mother."

Tracey grinned. "You're powerful, ya know that?" Tracey held up her hand to show that the leather had been melted away at the little girl's magic she had swiped through. I hadn't noticed it.

"We have to hurry," I whispered. There was no telling what was waiting for us outside.

The little girl nodded her head and all of the children followed out behind her. She grabbed Tracey's hand and we ran down the stairs. It was a long chain of children. My mother was going to have the best time with this. She loved children and I was bringing her an entire school of them.

Gabriel met us outside. "Good thing you're moving into your own home. The manor is going to need every bed and every room."

There was no way we were going to get all of these kids into the cars. I looked at Tracey out of the corner of my eye. "How are we going to transport all of them?"

There had to be at least fifty kids, maybe more following behind us into the woods. Tracey shrugged as she held two children's hands. "I'm going to have to figure out how much magic these kids know."

Sheeva's daughter grinned. "We know a lot more than you do, blood witch."

Tracey cocked her head in surprise but laughed all the same. "You know how to fit all of you into my SUV like a clown car?"

The little girl grinned. "I would love to."

The drive back to the Pack Lands was a cramped one. Somehow their magic had gotten all of them into each of our vehicles. We drove for hours too, just in case someone was following our trail. It didn't matter though. Unless the children could help Tracey figure out how to put a cloaking spell over the Pack Lands, they would know exactly where all the children went.

Getting all the children out of the vehicles was a different kind of difficult as they adjusted to being outside of the magic. One of the kids bent over at the waist to barf into the bushes. Another fell over complaining he was dizzy and a few others said their heads hurt.

Archer clapped me on the back and grinned. Tracey wrinkled her nose. "Why do you smell like a dumpster fire?"

Archer wrinkled his nose at her. "First, you always have to destroy evidence. I burned the building and the surveillance room. Most of the video cameras in the building were extremely outdated. They weren't being fed over wifi. I would imagine it was done that way so the kids couldn't be tracked over an IP address. But all the same, super stupid and overly confident on Damian's part. He will never know who took the kids."

Tracey shook her head. "I managed to mask our scents on the way out, thankfully."

Sheeva's daughter looked up at us. She was sitting on the front porch of the house. "We have been waiting for someone to rescue us. I've been sending out magical beacons for the last few months." Her shoulders fell. "I can help you cloak the entire property. I'll need a few ingredients and then we can walk the perimeter." As she spoke, I got the distinct impression she wasn't under the age of six. She had to be small for her age. She was entirely too smart. Tracey put her hand in the little girls and they walked toward Granny's.

What the hell was I supposed to do with all of these kids? They all watched me with their bright hair and wide eyes. No pressure.

"Hi, kids," I waved awkwardly. "What do you know about the place you were staying?"

A little boy in the front answered with a slight oriental accent. "We know everything about why we were there and taken from our families. We know we were being held to get our parents to obey an evil dick."

A few of the kids snickered in response. I pressed my palms into my eyes. "Uh, yes, to all of that."

My mom rolled her eyes from the doorway of the manor. Knox slapped me on the back with a "way to go" and Tracey shook her head from where I could see her disappearing into the woods. My mom took that opportunity to come out in her bathrobe and slippers. She looked like the perfect grandma besides the fact that she was flawless and hardly had any wrinkles. Being immortal was the best skincare regimen. "I'll take it from here. I'm Alice Crimson and I'm the Alpha's mother. We are doing our best to accommodate all of you and we are going to encourage that you don't use magic to try to contact your families. Things still aren't safe and we don't want to risk anything. Magic will be permitted because we know what it's like to trap a part of ourselves. Please only do it under supervision. I don't know how it was before but these are our rules to keep everyone safe. Especially the wolf pups that don't have magic."

A little girl raised her hand.

"Wolves have magic."

My mother raised her eyebrows. "What have they taught you about the wolves?"

She little girl grinned and her brown eyes shone. "Wolves are their own kind of magic. Magic from the goddess."

Knox nodded his head in appreciation. "I like these witches. We *are* blessed by the gods."

"This transition isn't going to be easy for our

pack or for you. Bear with us as we try to make all of you as comfortable as we can."

I met my mom halfway and wrapped my arms around her. She was the glue that kept the pack together and I couldn't help but hope that one day, Jade would be the same for us.

## CHAPTER 37
JADE

We had moved to the main house, where Damian was staying. Somehow the rest of the compound we had been living in had been set on fire too. I wondered if it was Micah's farewell gift. I knew he was gone for good as soon as he left. It hurt but I knew he had to get out. The plan had gone horribly wrong and I couldn't imagine living with that guilt.

Besides Bee, twelve others had died in the explosion because of the building falling on them or the fire. We were two of the lucky ones.

I tried to remind myself of that every time I looked at Lucas. He had suffered a bad head injury and a concussion but other than that he was fine. I had needed six stitches on the top of my head because the amount of wolfsbane in the air had been toxic. That was another reason four wolves had died. They had been too close to it when it exploded.

Lucas was laying on the plush canopy bed reading a magazine when our routine watch came through the door to do an inspection. He checked under the beds, behind the curtains, and in the bathroom before he marched out. He wore a ski mask and didn't speak to us. None of the guards were permitted to speak to us and now we hardly had a chance to be alone or speak quietly. If we got too close, a guard marched in to separate us. My skin crawled with the thought of it. There was nothing more I hated than Damian.

I had hated Rafe. I had hated how he had taken my choice away from me. I had hated his smirking face and his taunting. But now? Now all I hated was being under Damian's thumb and he enjoyed it too. He always wore a little knowing smile when I saw him. But he never asked. He never asked if I had planned the explosion until one evening when I was eating lunch on the balcony outside of my room. I had already checked to see if I could jump off of it, but it had a magical forcefield surrounding it.

I took a bite out of my sandwich as he came out. He sat in the metal patio chair beside me and we watched as the rain poured from the heavens and bounced off of the magic surrounding us. It was like we were in our own little bubble.

"Did you plan it?" His voice came out quiet, unsure.

"Plan what?" I asked confused. I really had no idea what he was talking about.

"The explosion?"

"No, I didn't. Everything about that day makes me sick."

A guard I hadn't realized was behind us spoke up. "Truth."

"What?" I asked.

"I brought a wolf with me to tell me if you were lying or not."

I nodded my head. It was to be expected and I was thankful that I hadn't been included in that day. I felt guilty enough over it. I shouldn't have tried anything or thought about trying anything when it meant another person would get hurt. Now I had several deaths on my hands, even if I wasn't the one that planned it. I chewed a few more bites of my sandwich before I placed my plate on the iron table between us. The wolfsbane coated my tongue and I had the urge to throw up all the food I had eaten. I was back to being fed wolfsbane with every meal.

Would this interrogation change anything? I doubted it, Damian was on edge. He was extra jumpy. A bird squawked in the distance and he about jumped out of his skin.

"Are you okay?" I asked as his head twitched.

He ran his hands down his thighs before he shot me a dazzling smile. "Yes, of course. There have just been some hiccups lately. Nothing I can't fix."

I nodded my head and watched the mountains. The previous day there had been deer feeding in the distance. This had become my happy place. Lucas didn't even bother me when I came out here to eat the poison they called meals.

I stayed out on the balcony until the sun dipped down and disappeared for the night. I tucked my legs beneath myself as the night grew chilly and I wished I had my sweater.

Right on cue, Lucas came out with a blanket. He wrapped it around my shoulders before he sat down beside me. "Do you think Micah is okay?"

It seemed like a safe enough question. I reached out between us and pulled his hand into mine. We threaded our fingers together and I shrugged. "I really don't know."

We lapsed back into a safe silence before he got up and scooted his chair closer to mine. He wrapped his arm around my shoulder and I snuggled into the crook of his arm. His warmth spread into me and I sighed in contentment. "Do you think we will be here forever?"

Lucas rested his chin on top of my head. "I think Damian will get bored of you by then."

"He mentioned that I have a mate," I hadn't said it out loud until that moment. I had a mate out there somewhere.

"I figured you did," He ran his hands over the tops of my arms. "All the best ones do."

I poked him in the ribs. "You have a mate out there too."

His chest vibrated with a hum. "I don't know. I would like to think so. Before I was a wolf, the thought of having a mate terrified me. Now the thought isn't so bad. Maybe it will be someone that is everything I'm not. Strong and courageous."

I rolled my eyes and poked him again. "You are those things."

He shrugged. "My dad never thought so."

"Axel is kind of an ass."

He let out a laugh before he said, "Shhhh. I'm sure he can hear you all the way over here."

"I hope he can." I cupped my hands around my mouth. "YOU'RE A SWOLLEN ASSHOLE AXEL."

He leaned over at the waist and choked on a laugh. "Swollen?" He let out a wheeze.

I shrugged. "I don't like the word fat."

He continued to laugh. "So you call him swollen? That is rich."

His laugh was infectious and eventually I was doubled over with him as we poked each other and giggled like maniacs. The best part of it? We weren't broken up by a stupid guard and we were allowed to live in that moment.

Lucas had left for breakfast already when a knock on the door woke me up. I was enjoying the ability to sleep in, especially with the wolfsbane in my system. It made me even more sleepy than usual. I rolled out of the bed and landed on the balls of my feet. I flopped my hair away from my face. I pulled the dark wooden door open and came face to face with Damian. He looked uncertain as I ran my fingers through my hair, trying to tame it.

"Hi," I breathed out behind my palm. I still

hadn't brushed my teeth and was sure my breath was nasty.

He smiled softly. "I didn't mean to wake you."

The soft tone of his voice made me nervous. He had been on edge lately but this was different. Damian was usually confident about everything he did, but today he didn't seem as sure of himself.

I shrugged my shoulders. "I'm up now, what's up?"

He looked down at my silk nightclothes and a blush tinged his cheeks. An actual *blush*. I cocked my head as I scrubbed a hand down my face. It was all I had to wear to bed. I imagined this had been one of his personal quarters at one point, meant to occupy *female* guests, judging by the clothing that was kept here. It was barely my size but I made it work. Poor Lucas had to have his clothes delivered every morning and I hated the commotion that happened with that. There was no point in making more trouble. I crossed my arms over my ample chest, self-conscious now.

"I was going to ask if you would come take a walk with me?" He ran a hand through his dark hair and for a moment, he was so breathtakingly handsome I couldn't stand it.

I nodded my head. "Yes, I would like that."

Even though I wasn't so sure if I would like it. The thought of him this nervous made my insides feel weird and not in a good way.

My movements were jerky as I yanked on jeans and a black t-shirt in the bathroom. My fingers were a bit more steady as I braided my hair over my shoulder. It was strange looking at myself without makeup. It had been weeks since I had worn it and I didn't really miss it anymore. My green eyes were brighter than they had ever been, even though the wolfsbane flooded thickly through my veins. My skin had never been clearer either.

Damian was rubbing his hands together when I walked into the hall. I didn't bother with locking my room. There was nothing in there that held any importance to me. I didn't have personal belongings or items that gave me nostalgia. All of that was at my home. My parents had called after the explosion and I tried to sound as calm as I could manage while we were all being herded into a new home. They didn't seem concerned as the connection kept cutting out anyway. The only thing that held importance to my life now was that phone and it was tucked safely in my back pocket.

Damian kept a good foot of distance between us as we walked down the heavily decorated halls. I had been stunned when Lucas and I had been led to the room we now shared. I hadn't expected to be kept in such lavish quarters but Damian was stretched thin as it was. It only made sense that his two most valuable assets were close to him. The rug that ran all the way down the hall was a deep burgundy that reminded me of spilled blood and the edges were decorated with gold tassels. On the walls, every few feet, were massive portraits of what looked to be important people. They were all dressed nicely and as we continued farther, I noticed the style of clothing changed drastically too.

"Did you know them?" I didn't know how long witches would live but I imagined it would be similar to a werewolf's life span.

He shook his head before he smiled ruthlessly. "No," He cleared his throat and reminded me of why he was the villain. "They were some rich snobs that stole from the poor, especially the witches in the coven nearby. I killed them nearly a decade ago and took this castle for myself before I really started to put my plan in action."

"They were human?"

I couldn't help but think of what Tracey's mother, Vivian, had told us. We were the guardians over the humans. We were here to help protect them against themselves and the other supernatural races that would do them harm.

He ran his tongue over his teeth as he looked at each painting we passed. "Deliciously so."

"I didn't think witches bothered with humans or eating them. I thought that was a wolf and vampire thing."

Damian laughed. "No, it's definitely a thing for every race. Supernatural or otherwise. The blood holds power that a witch can't get from anywhere else. It's rich in *life*. I only tasted it when I killed the people that owned this estate. It was the best experience of my life." His eyes flicked to mine. "I wish I hadn't poisoned my father and tasted his blood instead. The blood holds many secrets, as well as power."

## CHAPTER 38
JADE

Damian had gone through all the trouble of having a picnic set up for us in the field behind the massive estate. But no matter how thoughtful it was, I couldn't get over how twisted his mind was. His comment about his father made me think of Rafe. Except there were two drastic differences between the men. Damian had enjoyed killing his father, while Rafe didn't.

The food wasn't laced in wolfsbane, thankfully, but, I still couldn't enjoy it. All I could think about was that I wasn't a guest here. I was a prisoner and I didn't know how I had let myself forget that. Especially after how he had burned Bee's body without any flicker of emotion. Lucas had told me that night, as I was trying to fall asleep, that a witch needed to remain whole in the resting process or her magic wouldn't pass onto her offspring. It was why the Salem Witch Trials happened the way they did. They wanted to prevent the passing of one's power. If they had buried them, the remaining witches would have only gotten stronger.

Damian spoke very little as we ate and even less as we were walking back to his home. We were passing under an ornate brick archway when something didn't feel right. The vibe in the air changed slightly. Before I knew it, Damian had me pressed against the wall in the shadows. The brick pressed into the exposed skin on my arms and a breeze made a chill brush over my skin. Damian's fingers wrapped around my throat while he leaned in.

All I wanted to do was transform my hand into claws to rip his throat out. I couldn't breathe but he didn't care. His pupils were completely dilated as he looked at me beneath him.

"If you've been involved in the plan to take me from my throne, I will find out," he whispered. "I will find out and I will make you beg for death, do you understand?"

The pressure on my neck grew heavier until the breath was completely gone from my lungs. I nodded the best I could.

His fingers unwrapped from my neck and he took a step back. "Good, I'm glad we are on the same page." He ran a finger down my cheek and I flinched away. Not because I was afraid, but because I was disgusted. Disgusted that he could get away with this. "If you betray me, I will make sure you regret it."

He walked away before I could say or do anything. My hands trembled as I reached up to rub the sensitive skin there. With the wolfsbane still in my system, whatever marks he had left behind would still be present when I saw Lucas. I closed my eyes as I leaned back into the shadows and let the tears slip from my eyes.

The pain that shook my body wasn't from what he had done to me, but instead, how angry I was that I couldn't do anything back. My body shook with the frustration that I couldn't retaliate. I hastily wiped the tears from my face as I stewed over what Damian had said.

Had Micah been caught trying to defy Damian? Had he been caught planning or cleaning up the plan from the bomb? As much as I worried about him, I knew it was pointless to do so. There was nothing I could do while I was trapped here. Even so, he could take care of himself. He had proven that when he created the entire diversion and kept me out of it.

A shaky breath escaped me as I pushed away from the shadows and marched back to the house. None of us had been permitted to explore the castle but we were allowed to be on the grounds, outside. I hadn't bothered with trying to see what was out here on what seemed to be a hundred acres. I knew we were in the middle of nowhere. I had seen the massive winding drive that brought us to the compound out front that had to have been a servant housing at one point. I didn't know how I had missed this massive building behind it.

I rolled my eyes to myself.

*Magic, duh.*

Of course, he wouldn't want anyone to know the luxury he was living in, especially with the way we had been living. I couldn't imagine his followers being thrilled that he was living in a castle that could house all of them, but kept them on a leash in hell. I wondered what they thought of him now. Or was he wining and dining them so well that they no longer cared? I sighed. I had no business walking around the grounds or trying to make friends again. We were being watched closer than we had been before. I had no doubt that my tears would be reported back to Damian. He was looking for weakness and his men would find it.

Making friends only meant more heartache in a place like this. I couldn't watch any more people burn for me or Damian. I would stay far away from them if it meant keeping them safe. Especially Lucas. He got joy from exploring the grounds and hiking each day with a supervisor nearby but I couldn't stomach it. I couldn't handle the thought of enjoying anything here. All Damian would do was exploit it.

Lucas's smile flashed through my thoughts. Pain seared my chest. I knew the time would come when Damian would use him against me. I was just too damn selfish to do anything to prevent that heartache. I couldn't give up Lucas even if I wanted to and that was what scared me the most.

## CHAPTER 39
RAFE

What now? I couldn't help but ask myself that daily since we had rescued the kids and we waited. What we were waiting for, I wasn't exactly sure. Micah said we were waiting for a sign from the witches. I pinched the bridge of my nose. I was getting increasingly frustrated with *waiting*.

At least the kids were free and adjusting well to the new environment they had been thrown in. Most of them were in elementary school so they went to class with the younger pups in the pack. They took everything that was happening with a smile. Micah watched them daily to make sure they were adjusting okay too. I could see the worry in his eyes and body language. One of the children had lost their mother and yet, he hadn't told me which one and he hadn't told the child either. He refused to get too close, even though he watched them.

Micah shook his head as we walked from the manor's porch. "You don't understand. We can't just attack. He has the most powerful witches in his employ and I don't think they know the kids were saved. We would have heard from them by now. They would have risen up. Plus he has an army of wolves."

Knox rolled his eyes. "We have…" He smacked his lips together reconsidering. "We have two witches and a bunch of kids."

Tracey's eyes rolled to the heavens as Archer snickered. "You should probably still be in school with the children."

Mav shook his head before he shoved his hands into the pockets of his jeans. "Micah is right, we can't go in there claws out and think we are going to win with just the few of us."

Micah scratched his cheek. "You don't understand, this isn't to *win*. We aren't going in there to win anything. We would be going there to get Jade out, that's it."

Gabriel pressed his lips together in a thin line. "I don't like that idea. There are others in there that need help too."

Micah let out an exasperated sigh. "The more people we try to save, the worse this will go. It's only Jade or I don't agree to help."

The man was starting to get on my nerves. He knew Jade was my mate and I was Alpha, yet he kept trying to call all the shots. I didn't mind more ideas but he wouldn't take anything else into consideration.

"Let's go to the war room," I looked at all the people in my pack as we walked down to the path to my building. "There are too many ears."

In the center of my war room was a massive round table. When I was a child I had always imagined it as King Arther's round table. All the important things happened there. We hadn't sat at the table while we were planning before but I was too tired to stand around or sit at the bar.

Tracey gasped as I pulled the first leather chair out. I sat down, the weariness in my body followed. I could have slept there if I had come alone. "I feel like this is a pivotal moment." Her voice held awe.

She ran her fingers over the top of a chair across from me before she reverently sat down. Maybe sitting at this table, where my father and his advisors had sit would instill some kind of respect in the rowdy men I loved to hate.

Micah looked around at all of my men and stayed standing until they had all sat down. He was showing them his own kind of respect as he realized this was an important day for my friends. They had grown up watching my father's men as well. They knew how special this place was to me. He could probably feel it in the air.

Micah leaned forward in his chair. "My plan is rather simple and I have a feeling you won't like it."

My men and Tracey remained silent as he continued. "I am the only one that knows the ins and outs of his estate. I would go in, go to see Damian, and then get her out in the middle of the night. I would possibly need one person as backup or two waiting outside."

"You're right," I leaned back and pinned him with a dark stare. "I don't like it. But I also know I can't get caught in that place if I'm what he's after."

"Knox and Archer will go with you." I nodded to each of them. I hated saying it. "I'll stay behind."

Micah looked at the two men that were going to accompany him. "We will not be saving any others. The only one that matters is Jade. If you try to get away from that plan or try to go against me, I will leave you in the den of monsters."

## CHAPTER 40
JADE

The bruising on my neck had gotten worse just like I thought it would. Lucas came in from his hike and immediately skidded to a stop. "I leave for one afternoon and something has happened."

I had thought about hiding it but I knew it would be no use. He would find out eventually. I finished off the chocolate pudding I had been snacking on. "It's not a big deal."

"You sound like a domestic abuse case and what's worse? You look like one too." He toed his shoes off before he climbed onto the bed next to me. His jaw ticked as he looked me over. "Is this all that happened?"

I nodded. What was I to say? There was no need to explain anything. We both knew Damian was the bad guy here, we had just forgotten how bad he was. He could have hurt me much worse.

"I see that look in your eye, Jade." His voice cracked. "He's not going to stop now. He put his mark on you. It will happen again."

My anger got the best of me. Maybe it was because I wasn't used to someone being so protective that wasn't my parents but it reared its ugly head. "This isn't the worst thing that has ever happened to me. You think Rafe was the first bad boy I had a run-in with? You think other guys didn't beat me around?"

Lucas took a step away from me and his face fell. "Just because that happened to you doesn't mean you deserve it."

I closed my eyes as I felt the burning there intensify. "I know what I deserve now, but I want you to understand that I can handle this."

He pressed his forehead against mine. "You're playing with bigger monsters here, Jade."

"Good thing I'm a monster too."

## CHAPTER 41
TRACEY

Was this how my brother had felt when he was here? Like an outsider? I had always been an outsider with him, but now it was different. I was different. The world around me was different. Trying to make sense of it all just confused me further.

The pack was scared of me. I could see it on their faces, in their auras, and smell it in the air. The witch and the wolf. The only ones that didn't see me that way were Rafe and the guardians. They still treated me the same, even though it was sometimes annoying. I was thankful for some bit of normalcy while I tried to get my bearings through all of this. It felt next to impossible but I held my chin up higher as I walked to Granny's.

Carden was waiting for me at the front of the house. Today he was watering her garden. He shot me a sweet smile before he looked back down at his duties.

The rest of the pack didn't want him here any more than they wanted me or the witch children running around. Though the witch children had started to grow on them more than I had or Carden. Some of the wolves were older than even Granny. Their immortality had served their bodies well but not their brains. They refused to grow in their thinking or understanding. Granny seemed to be the only progressive one out of the bunch.

"Good morning, Carden," I tried to not sound grumpy. It wasn't his fault he was here. But he helped Granny more than anyone else did and I knew that she appreciated him being around.

He bowed his head. "Good morning, Tracey, how are you feeling?" I tried to blink past the bright gold strands weaving around him but it was no use. No matter what Granny taught me about blocking auras and magic in the air wasn't working. It was like my brain and wolf were entirely too stubborn. But I had faith in Granny. She was here in this pack for a reason. She had helped all of us since we were pups.

I waved my hand dismissively. "I'm feeling fine, thank you."

The wood on the door was worn beneath my hand as I pushed it open. The first thing I noticed was the smell of artificial Mac & cheese cooking. I scrunched my nose in disgust. My granny would never. But when I turned around the corner in the hallway, toward the kitchen, I saw the culprit behind the fake cheese fiasco. My mother would have a fit. Mac & cheese was better when it was made from scratch. Granny had been the one that had taught her that.

A little blonde girl stood on a chair beside the stove while Granny twirled her finger in the air beside it. The spoon spun lazily in the pot. The little girl watched in awe. It was a party trick I knew well from when I was a child. Granny had always cooked with her magic. It was the one thing I had missed as I had gotten older.

They both turned to me at the same time. It wasn't an unusual thing for the witch kids to be around her cottage, but not many were brave enough to step foot inside. Older witches and their strong auras were known to scare children off. I knew that all too well with my own brother. He had been terrified of Granny as he had grown into his power.

The little girl had the audacity to turn her nose up at me. "And who are you?"

I barked out a laugh. "Excuse me?"

The child hopped down from the stool and pinned me with an indifferent stare. "Your aura is strange. It's not like the rest of the witches."

Then in my mind. *"Why are you so different? What is it? What can I find in your head?"*

I slammed down the mental wards Granny had taught me to put up. She blinked rapidly. "I wasn't finished."

"If you don't learn some manners, you'll be tossed out onto your head and the last thing you'll be worried about is other people's minds," I snarled.

"Already going head to head with the little she-devil, I see," Carden said from the doorway.

I had to calm the wolf inside of me. "You could have warned me."

"And miss that look on your face? I don't think so. She's a spitfire, isn't she?" Carden leaned against the doorframe and grinned.

The little girl's brown eyes watched him just as

warily as they watched me. "My name is Valentina, not spitfire."

"It's nice to meet you Valentina, but if you don't stay out of my head, you'll learn to regret it."

Granny lifted her eyebrow at the small girl. "You heard her." Her eyes moved to mine. "We are working on her manners and the use of consent. She isn't used to either. In the hell they were kept in, she had to use her magic to protect the other children. She would rifle through memories to see who was a friend and who was foe."

My lips twisted. "Don't forget, I'm the one that rescued you."

Valentina smiled softly. "I will not forget but I know not everyone is to be trusted."

Granny grinned. "She is only worried about self-preservation." She ran her hand down the girl's straight blonde hair. "Fix yourself some lunch and we will begin our lessons. I have requested a few grimoires from the archives. I should be able to help you with this unusual and incredible magic." She winked.

Granny motioned me to follow her. Carden bowed his head to her as we passed. "I'll try to keep her out of trouble."

"I don't think you'll be enough to do that," I muttered.

Granny snickered and I felt this overwhelming emotion inside of my chest. The kind of emotion that makes you want to hug the other person.

"Who is the kid?" I asked when we got to the tree line that split my Granny's cottage from my parents' property. She wasn't a wolf so she wasn't permitted to own land with the pack but my parents had given her enough land to do what she needed then planted enough trees to give her the privacy she craved after my grandfather passed away.

"Her mother was the one that sacrificed herself so the kids could be found," My heart was immediately in my throat. "She will have nowhere to go. I can't find a coven that has mind jumpers."

"Mind jumpers?"

Granny sighed. "Yes, she can take over a person's mind, read their thoughts, and go through their memories. She is a rare witch. No coven will take her in when the children go back to their parents. They will be too afraid of what she is, what she can do."

I frowned. "And you won't be afraid?"

Granny smiled. "No, she is no worse than you or your brother. Her power is different, not bad. I am doing what I can to teach her about it. If I can find another like her, it would help but I don't think there are any."

"Must you always take on the outsiders?" My mind immediately went to Carden. He had been offered a place in the pack, he had sworn to the Alpha, but he had stayed glued to my grandmother all the same.

"The only way that child will be dangerous is if she doesn't know love. When she finds out what happened to her mother, there is no telling how she will react. She is going to need allies in this world. I don't think she was ever with a coven before they forced her with all of these children."

I pressed my hands against my face. "She hasn't told you?"

Granny shrugged. "Why would she? She owes me nothing."

I shook my head. "Fine, but you need to get more information on her before this becomes more permanent."

Granny lifted one eyebrow in contempt. "Are you telling me this as my granddaughter or someone with higher authority in the pack?"

I clenched my jaw. "I don't know why I'm

telling you at all. She's dangerous, so just be careful."

Granny touched my jaw and forced me to look at her. "If you think I haven't faced off with her kind before, then you would be naive. I have come across much more danger in my entire life than that child. I faced off against the pack you love so dearly. I took down an entire army when the witches of my first coven were hunted. I have evaded spies, the mafia, and plenty of other magic races that are now long gone."

"Why do you care so much?" My throat was thick. I didn't know why I cared so much. What was the child to me? Nothing. There was a whisper in the back of my head that said she would take my granny from me. It was jealousy rearing its ugliness. Granny noticed it at the same time I did. Her brows softened and she took a step closer to me. She held her hands out and I was immediately in her arms. She smelled like lavender and mint today. Thankfully there was none of that fake cheese smell clinging to her.

"I care because I see you and your brother in her eyes." Her voice broke as she held me. "I see a child that needs me, needs us. I don't know why I feel connected to her like I do but I know she will bring change to the witch community."

I pulled back slightly. "What is wrong with the witches?"

Granny pressed her lips together. "There are many things wrong with them. They live on power highs. They no longer care if the world knows what they are. We once lived in secret for a reason but now most of them are getting caught. Either they want to be caught or they don't know any better."

"But that doesn't concern us." I tried to reason with her.

Granny raised both brows this time. "You don't think so? What do you think will happen when the witches are captured or they are all gone?" She poked my chest. "You will be hunted next. My own children and grandchildren will face another war, another witch trials. I can't stand to see history repeat itself but it will."

"Can't the council of the witches keep them from doing this?"

Granny took a deep breath. "The council of witches has been gone for a long time. The archives lay empty. Something is coming and I don't want you to have to face it alone."

**CHAPTER 42**
JADE

Damian didn't come around again since his angry outburst. I didn't expect him to but there were whispers around the grounds that he was finally losing it. That something big had happened and now he felt like he was losing the game. I listened as intently as I could but with the wolfsbane still in my system, it was hard to hear. Getting too close to the other wolves was not a good idea either.

I was walking back to our room when I heard the first crash. I ducked down low and crawled to the wall. My arms were overstretched above my head, afraid one of the cinderblocks in the ceiling would crush me if this was an attack. But after a few minutes, there wasn't another and I stood up carefully. My knees wobbled as I made my way to our door. Just a few more steps and I would be there.

Another crash had me diving for the floor again. This time the crashing was followed by the ground shaking and loud screaming. Except it wasn't screams of terror or fear. These were screams of rage. I crawled across the floor when I heard the shout clear as day.

"You let them escape!" Damian's roar rattled the doors.

There was a whimper before a door down the hall slammed open and a person went hurtling out of the room. He smashed into the wall with a sickening thud. He rolled into a heap on the floor before he tried to stand up. His legs shook as he took a step forward but it didn't matter. A blast of light came from the bedroom and all that was left of the man after a few seconds was a pile of ash. There wasn't even enough time to be shocked or horrified. One minute he was there, then the next he was gone. I didn't bother with getting off of the floor as I crawled the rest of the way to the bedroom. I don't know how I managed to open the door or even get into the bed. All I remembered was waking up the next morning with Lucas rubbing my back in soothing circles.

"Three witches are gone," he whispered into the darkness.

I leaned over the side of the bed and my stomach emptied onto the rug. I didn't know what caused it. Maybe it was the horror over what was happening. Maybe it was Nalia's ruthlessness being gone. I had killed two wolves without blinking. Who was this girl vomiting on the carpet?

"I'm no better than he is," I whispered when I was done throwing up. My voice shook and my throat ached but somehow the words made it out.

He clucked his tongue. "That isn't true. You took care of people that were evil. He is killing people that are innocent. He is a *murderer*. Those wolves would have killed you if you hadn't killed them. You have to establish a pack dynamic. Even here. You're the Alpha."

His words didn't make me feel any better. In fact, they made me feel worse.

"Alpha?" I choked on the word.

"You established that dominance here. Damian doesn't have that. He doesn't have a wolf. All he has is fear."

. . .

It only got worse. Every single person walked on eggshells. The witches that came to clean up the vomit didn't even bother with taking the rug out. They caught it on fire. The breeze from the balcony took away the smoke and ash while we waited for them to finish. They were too afraid of how he would react to my vomit. He would take it out on them. We all knew it. They shook in fear as they cleaned the bathroom. The toilet brush clanging against the toilet was the only indicator that they were scared out of their minds. I was sure Damian was playing roulette with who would be next. We all waited on pins and needles.

I hadn't gotten out of bed when the door splintered open. I clutched the blankets to my chest as Lucas flew out of the bathroom with his toothbrush still in his mouth. Damian stood in the now bare doorway. Crisscross scars marked his bare chest and pajama pants were low on his hips. His eyes were wide and glassy. He didn't wait for me to get out of bed, instead, he marched to where I was and pulled me from the blankets. He didn't care about what I was wearing. His eyes didn't take in how indecent I was. All he cared about was dragging me out of the room. His grip around my wrist caused me to wince as I stumbled behind him down the hall.

Lucas raced behind us. I shook my head ferociously. I could fight him off. I wasn't starving myself, even if the wolfsbane was strong within me. I worked out in our room every night. I did pull-ups and sit-ups in the bathroom doorway. I tried my best to keep my strength up for the moment he came for me.

"Where are you taking her?" Lucas shouted behind us. At least he had stopped following. I could try to protect myself but I didn't know if I could protect Lucas. Damian didn't bother with answering, he only picked up his pace. When we hit the stairwell, that's where I didn't fare too well. My legs collapsed under me with just about every step. When Damian was over my struggles, he stopped before he yanked me over his shoulder. I yelped as he went down the stairs at a much faster pace. My hair had fallen out of its bun and was now a curtain in front of my face.

We kept descending and with all the jostling and hair in my face, I couldn't see where we were going. Only that the light in the room kept getting dimmer.

Between the smell and the darkness, I knew nothing good would come out of this. Why hadn't I fought while he was trying to get me down the stairs? Why had I just gone with him?

*Because he would have taken it out on Lucas.* A voice whispered in my mind. I fought back a shiver as my body slid from his shoulder. We were in a dungeon of some sort. The smell of blood and mildew hit me. I had to fight everything in me to not throw up again. What had he been doing down here? The smells were too fresh for this to be an old forgotten place.

## CHAPTER 43
JADE

When I had thought Damian had gotten worse, I had no idea just how much. Or maybe he hadn't gotten worse at all. Maybe this was who he had been hiding.

I lifted my chin and stared him down. If he was going to kill me, then I wasn't going to go down without a fight. I wasn't going to let him take my dignity too. He had already taken so much from me. "What did I do now?"

He didn't acknowledge me. Instead, he whispered like a madman to himself. I could hardly distinguish what he was saying until I heard, "They will come for her next. They got the kids out. This is their next stop. I can't let them take her."

My heart leapt into my throat. Had Micah managed to help my pack get the kids out? While he was focused on his muttering. I took a look at my surroundings. The barred door was wide open. He dragged his fingers through his hair and made it stand up. I took a deep breath before I took off running. If the kids had made it out then I didn't need to worry about the witches. We could get out. They could band together. All I needed to do was tell them. But as soon as my foot passed over the threshold, he had his hand wrapped around my hair. My entire body jerked backward as lightning lit up the back of my skull.

Pain blossomed in my tailbone as it connected with the damp brick flooring. I wheezed as he yanked harder on my hair. I had no doubts that he had taken chunks of it out of the back of my head. I scrambled backwards on the cobblestones but it was no use. He only continued to pull harder.

"If you thought you could escape, the jokes are on you." His voice didn't sound as crazed. It sounded almost clear. I wrapped my fingers around his wrist and tried to get some kind of relief but his grip was too firm.

A cry escaped my lips as he threw me down onto the ground. Damian leaned over me and smiled. His eyes were clear and that's what scared me the most.

"What do you want from me?" Pride swelled within my chest at my steady voice. I honestly didn't know how I managed it. My head ached and there was a warm trickle down the back of my neck that worried me.

"What I have always wanted from you, I have wanted Rafe Crimson but you have yet to deliver him to me." He tilted his head before he smiled. "Except I don't want him anymore. I want you. I have wanted you since I wrapped my fingers around your neck. I had thought I wanted to take you so Rafe would come to me. But now I want what's his. I will not let him come in here and get you."

"I belong to no man," I snarled.

"I will break you of that, like I broke all the others. Do you smell their blood down here? Can you hear the phantom echoes of their screams?"

I sat up straighter on the floor. "You will have to kill me. Do you understand me? You will never own me. You will never have any piece of me. Not now, not ever."

Pain bloomed on the side of my face and darkness kissed my eyes.

. . .

When I came to, there was a small fluorescent bulb hanging above me. There wasn't anyone in the room and I was spread out on a metal table. Every single horror movie I had seen growing up didn't make this situation any better. I squeezed my eyes closed as I tried to think of anything that would help me get out. Horror movies had been my jam growing up. There had to have been something in them that would have prepared me to escape from this moment. But the longer I thought about it, the more I started to panic.

Leather restraints kept my wrists pinned to the table on either side of me. Thankfully I was still wearing the nightgown but it didn't cover much. My legs were also strapped down to the table and from what I could see, my feet were raw.

The back of my head still ached but the front of my head ached worse. Why hadn't I fought harder?

"I'm glad you're awake," Damian said from the shadows of the doorway. "Now we can talk."

I yanked on the bindings but they were too secure. Even all of my training wasn't enough to fight this. The wolfsbane definitely didn't help. Why hadn't I starved myself? Why had I been so compliant?

"Many years ago, I was born of a wolf and a witch. Much like your friend Lucas. My mother was killed in a war that my father started. He was foolish and didn't care about what would happen to those in his pack. After the war, he found his true mate. The one that his soul called to. My mother was forgotten and in turn, so was I. He sent me to live with witches. Living with wolves wasn't good for a son that never got one. I was a disgrace to him. After all, his firstborn would eventually take up the mantle of Alpha. But I couldn't do that. After I went to live with the witches, he never spoke to me again. I wrote him letters weekly. Sometimes daily. All I wanted was my father's approval. The letters were all returned. I thought it was because I was a witch. I began experimenting on myself. But it didn't matter, a wolf never chose me. A wolf chose every single witch and mortal I put it in, but never me."

"And that's why you're doing this?" I coughed.

Damian took a step farther into the room. "No, I do this because I want revenge for everything I ever wanted and will never get. But I'll have to break you first. I'll have to rip your wolf from you and then mate her to me."

Horror clouded my vision. *No.*

He took a step closer to me and ran the tip of a blade down my arm. Blood immediately bubbled up from the wound. I couldn't feel the pain as I fought the restraints. All that mattered was getting out. I would feel it later, but now, it didn't matter.

There was a slight stinging pain as he did the same to the other arm. I watched with rage as the blood spilled from my arms. He was still shirtless with his scars on display.

"What happened to you?" Maybe I could stall.

He stopped with the knife and looked down at himself. "This is what it takes to merge with a wolf that doesn't want you. Over fifteen different venoms from different packs. This is what I was left with. I was shredded from the inside out as the wolves wouldn't choose me. Do you know how painful that is?"

I could imagine. My first transformation hadn't been sunshine and daisies.

His pupils widened as he twirled the knife between his fingers. "Do you think I can cut your wolf out?"

He ran the knife up my thigh. This time and instead of fighting him, I rolled my head to the side and threw up again. It splattered his chest with a sickening sound as he tried to leap away from it. But he couldn't escape how sick he made me feel.

His retaliation was quick as his hand shot out and darkness took me over once again.

## CHAPTER 44
RAFE

Ford was helping me put down flooring in the master bathroom when I got the call. I hated cellphones and their insistent ringing but I had to keep one for appearances and sometimes if the pack couldn't get in touch through our link.

"Yes?" My shoulder kept the phone up against my ear as I helped guide my brother with the tiles.

"She's gone," Micah's voice was flat.

"Who?" I frowned as I stood up to walk away from my brother.

"Jade. Someone got a text to me a few minutes ago."

"Can we trust it?" I didn't want to trust it but there was a feeling in my gut that I never ignored. The feeling was telling me that she was gone. But I didn't want to accept it. If I did, that meant I was back at the drawing board.

"I'm not sure, but we will need to go in regardless. We have to at least notify them that the children are safe."

I ran my hand down the back of my neck. "Do you think they'll believe us?"

"I don't know," he sighed.

"We're going to figure it out, it just changes things slightly. We will do a recon and find her." *I hope.*

Ford's eyes were sad as he looked up from the tiles. "She's going to be okay?"

I shrugged as I hung up. "I don't know, but I will bring her back here. I promised everyone that and I promise you that now. I will do whatever it takes."

Ford set his jaw. "Show them no mercy."

## CHAPTER 45
JADE

The pain in my limbs was overwhelming. Shifting to and from my wolf the first few times wasn't this bad. The scent of copper was heavy in the air. I knew it was because he had been carving me up while I had been unconscious. I could feel the blood caked over my skin.

I didn't understand the man. Didn't someone torture someone because they wanted them to react? All this time, I hadn't been able to. Was he waiting to see how I would take what he had done to me? Curiosity got the best of me as I promised myself I wouldn't react to what he had done. I wouldn't give him the satisfaction. I knew he was watching me from the shadows, waiting to see how I would scream or cry. But truth be told, all I wanted to do was throw up on him again. The pain in my head had been worth that.

Right in the middle of my stomach was a massive *D* carved into the creamy skin. Except now, it wasn't creamy or even white. It was bright red with my blood. It looked like the wound was still bleeding and I wondered if I would die here. If I would bleed out. I leaned my head back and closed my eyes. I didn't bother with looking at the rest of the damage he had done. He had marked me and that was the worst he could do.

Right on cue, he stepped from the darkness. "No stitches on hand, but I have something just as effective."

He held up a longer thicker blade than the others. After a few seconds, it started to glow. Whether it was from all the trauma to my head or all the blood loss, it had taken me entirely too long to grasp that he was heating the metal with his magic. He leaned forward with a grin before he pressed the hot metal to my flesh. My back shot off the table as I bucked through the pain. A scream tore through my lips as the fiery heat only got worse on my middle. My chest heaved as saliva spilled from my lips and tears tumbled down my cheeks.

What felt like hours later, he pulled the smoking

blade from my stomach and smiled. "That wasn't too bad, was it?"

My mouth had pooled with saliva, as well as rolling down my neck. I leaned to the side as much as I could with my stomach screaming in protest as I spat what was left in my mouth at the man. His nostrils flared as he took a step back. My throat ached as I laid my head back down on the table and waited for him to hit me again. I hoped this time it killed me. Except the blow never came. He didn't bother with wiping the spit from his face either. He merely disappeared while I came to terms with my new branding.

🐾

### Rafe

My chest heaved as I shot up in bed and ripped my shirt from my back. I was sleeping in Jade's cottage. It was the only place that was complete enough for me. I felt odd sleeping in her bed that she hadn't even seen yet but I had nowhere else to go.

I rubbed the sensitive skin on my belly before I leaned over to turn the bedside table on. Right there in the middle of my stomach was a fading *D*.

It looked like someone had scratched into my skin, but it was fading too quickly.

Thankfully I kept the stupid cellphone close by. I took a picture of it just before it disappeared completely.

*Come to Jade's cottage immediately.*

There was only one thing that could do this to me and I hoped I wasn't right about it. The inside of my stomach still ached, even as the mark was gone. I didn't bother with trying to pull a shirt back on, the pain was still too bad.

Mav was the first one at the door. I held onto the frame to keep myself steady. Mav took one look at me before his hands transformed into claws and he crouched low in a defensive stance. I shook my head.

"No, the threat isn't here."

Knox, Archer, and Gabriel were next. They took one look at me before they did the same as Mav. Mav still hadn't relaxed.

I showed them the picture as I held my aching stomach. Knox's eyes grew dark as his wolf rose to the surface. "What does this mean? Is magic involved?"

"Yes and no," Granny said from the doorway. "There is magic but it is ancient mate magic. You are feeling what Jade is going through. There aren't many bonds strong enough that allow the other person to feel like this. You haven't claimed her and you're feeling this." Granny shook her head. She was wearing a robe with rubber boots. She took a step inside then got comfortable on Jade's couch. "Because you two haven't claimed each other yet, this leaves me to believe that a powerful witch is involved."

"How did you know to be here?" Knox leaned forward as he narrowed his eyes.

She swatted at him. "I could feel the magic going over the wards. The witch is using your mate bond to let you know that your mate is being tortured."

Rage like no other filled my mind. I stood up and my wolf rose to the surface. "I will tear the witch limb from limb."

Knox smacked my face. It only managed to get me out of the rage haze for a second. "We will get her, but you can't go in there like this. You can't go in there at all. Let us bring her home."

The rage faded to something else and before I knew it, I was choking back a sob. He had carved a *D* into her stomach. My guardians grouped around me as they each put their hands on my shoulders.

They were offering me their strength, their loyalty, and their compassion. The anger and revenge that had been so prevalent before, slowed down to a simmer. My shoulders collapsed under the weight of my own emotions at war.

Knox was the first to pull me into a hug. He patted my back affectionately before Archer came in for one. Before I knew it, I was in the biggest hug pile of my life.

"We will fight this war beside you. We will bring your mate home. Trust us to bring justice to you and Jade." I didn't know who said it but I swore I felt a few tears escape my eyes before we all pulled away.

Granny stood up from the couch. She tucked her hand inside of mine. "I will do my best to track the magic that is at work here, but I have no promises. I will do my best."

She kissed my cheek before she departed. My men were on her heels. Mav turned around at the last second. "Do you need me to stay?"

My entire life emotions hadn't been something I let many people see. My guardians had seen it all. They had seen my grief, rage, uncertainty, and lust. I couldn't say that they had seen me love because I didn't know what that felt like. But I knew they would see it eventually. I nodded my head. He grinned before he launched himself at the couch.

The poor piece of furniture groaned before a loud crack split the room and the couch collapsed on the floor. I didn't think it was possible but his bronze skin drained of all color.

"Don't tell Tracey," he whispered.

A laugh escaped my lips and it sounded so weird in the moment. My mate was going through unimaginable pain and I was able to laugh. It felt wrong. Guilt slammed into me as my face fell.

Mav winced. "I'll buy a new one."


Tracey would hold him to it too. I nodded my head and walked down the hall. The worst part of all of this wasn't the pain I had felt. It was the pain knowing there was absolutely nothing I could do to protect my mate. The pain in knowing there was no way I could soothe her.

## CHAPTER 46
JADE

Magic coated my tongue when I woke up the next day, or what I imagined to be the next day. I didn't have any windows or doors to tell me how much time had passed. My throat was thick as I tried to swallow. All of the screaming and crying I did had left me with an aching throat and a throbbing head. But those things didn't ache anywhere near the amount that the rest of my body did. It felt like I had been burned alive. There wasn't an inch of skin that didn't throb. My wrists were probably some of the worst of the damage too, based on how much I had thrashed against the bindings. The leather was too hard and unforgiving for my skin.

My stomach growled and I squeezed my eyes closed harder. Damian was anything but predictable but I knew that he wasn't going to let me eat. I hated that I hadn't been starving myself. I hated that I hadn't been more careful. I should have seen all of this coming. He wasn't going to leave me alone, he wasn't going to leave me be. As I sunk back into the oblivion of my mind, I wondered if maybe it was better if I just died down here.

## CHAPTER 47
RAFE

My anger was getting the best of me. A rumbled rattled the room as I slammed my hands down on the table. "I will not leave her there any longer! Do you understand me?"

Micah winced at the octave of my voice and probably my Alpha order washing over the rest of the room. "Yes, but I don't think this is the right time. If he has linked magic to draw you out, then we are playing right into his hands."

A sense of urgency slammed into my chest. I couldn't control it anymore. My eyes closed on their own accord.

Tracey rubbed my back for a moment before she spoke up. Ever since that night in the forest, she was different. She didn't speak immediately but instead, observed the room. She wasn't the bright, fun light we had all been used to either. Her enthusiasm was sucked away the night Jade was taken. The rest of her light was stolen when she was gifted her magic or it was awakened. We weren't exactly sure what had happened that night in the woods.

Granny assumed the magic was always inside of her but it laid dormant. It was the poison spells that had awakened the magic to protect her. Either way, she wasn't the same girl she was before. A part of me was sad about it, but I knew she had an interesting journey ahead of her and that was why she hadn't been my second yet. I didn't push for it because I knew she needed time. She needed to discover herself, and now, her magic.

"Rafe is right, regardless of his personal feelings clouding his judgment. We can't allow her to go through unnecessary pain there. The children are free, we simply need to get in then get out. We can even tell the witches while we are there that the kids are free, I don't know." Tracey sighed. "But we have to do something. We have to at least try."

Micah gritted his teeth together before his shoulders slumped in defeat. "Fine, but you aren't going to go in there to get her. We stick to the original plan. Rafe, you have to stay here."

## CHAPTER 48
TRACEY

By the time all of my knives were strapped to my legs and waist, the Guardians were ready to go. They took longer to get ready than any body else I had ever met. Women included. I slipped my hood over my honey-colored hair and prowled into the clearing behind the manor. I could make out the broken sofa through the window to Jade's cottage.

My lips thinned out as I pressed them together. Each man wore a stoic expression and tonight wasn't the night to try to find out who had done it. That could wait. Even though I did want to put a knife in the big oaf that did it.

I rolled my shoulders, then my neck as the Guardians strolled in. Micah wasn't dressed for combat, but I imagined he didn't have to be. He could walk into the place. The only thing that would hinder his story of kidnapping was that he looked too good.

My blade sang through the air before it sank thickly into his shoulder. The force of it knocked him back a few steps before he yanked the knife out of his skin. He hissed as it went. Blood poured from the wound before the skin started to stitch itself back together.

Knox had his fingers wrapped around my throat before I could pull another knife out. "What the hell are you doing?"

I grinned as his fingers tightened. "There is one flaw in your plan."

Rafe growled across the small area. "Release her." His demand cracked through the air like a whip. Knox immediately dropped his hand but he didn't step away from me. He took a step closer. His pupils were completely blown and there wasn't any color left in them. This was what happened when they hunted. I inched closer to him, answering the challenge. With Rafe I couldn't stare him down, it hurt too much. Knox? I could do it until my eyes fell out. His lips twisted into a wicked grin.

"What's the flaw, Tracey?" Rafe broke our stare down.

I cleared my throat and took a step back but I didn't break eye contact. I wouldn't show weakness. Not to Knox. I spoke while I stared into his eyes. "If Micah goes in there, Damian isn't going to trust that we didn't hold him hostage. He might not be a wolf but he has more than enough wolves to smell us on him. He needs to look the part or he's going to be very suspicious."

Rafe nodded and my next knife lodged into Micah's other shoulder with a sickening crunch. Micah grunted as he pulled this one out. Mav leaned over and his fist shot across Micah's face. Rafe was the only one that winced.

There was something seriously wrong with us.

Somehow the plan continued to change from the moment we were done beating Micah senselessly. He was bloodied and bruised. Unfortunately for him, we had to give him wolfsbane to make any injuries stick, so that meant they hurt pretty badly too. He was also stuffed into my trunk and knocked out cold. Thankfully the wolf had given us directions to this place before we knocked him out. We had to be believable, if not thorough.

The gravel crunched under my tires as we

neared the estate. There wasn't much nervous energy in my car. More adrenaline than anything else. I had managed to block most of the electric energy in my vision so I could drive. Granny had explained one too many times that powerful witches sometimes couldn't control seeing the golden threads in the world around them. Because of this, many of them had drivers, but in the witch community... the more power you have, the more influence, which means more money. Granny was a powerful witch but she had given it all up for my grandfather. She had given it all up for love. I could empathize with that but I couldn't understand it. I had never loved. I had never had the urge to find it. Being a dominant female wolf didn't make it easy to find a date, and now I had *witch* to add to the resume. Knox's black motorcycle came to a stop on the passenger side of my car.

He couldn't just be hot, he had to have all the hot accessories to go with. He slammed his booted feet to the earth and I tried to ignore the desire that rolled through me. I sighed. He was the most annoying man on the planet and I found him hot. I had always found him hot but I had managed to ignore it enough so he wouldn't scent my desire in the air.

Well, actually, I didn't want anyone to smell it. That was the most frustrating thing about being a wolf. Something that most wolves learned to ignore, but the Guardians? They were still in their prime. They loved to know that the women wanted them and I hated that the most. Mav was right behind him on his bike then Archer pulled up in his black SUV a few seconds later.

Knox kicked open my trunk and the desire I felt went away quickly. I frowned as I slammed my car door. "Can you be more gentle?"

Knox rolled his head my way and raised a brow. "Why would I do that? We have a prisoner in here."

"The prisoner isn't my car," I pressed my lips together as I rolled my hand for him to hurry up. Micah immediately jumped from the back and rammed his head into Knox's nose. I couldn't keep the smirk off of my face as blood sprayed. Micah hardly made it a few feet before Mav threw his massive body onto him and tackled him to the ground.

Micah jerked his shoulders around while Mav forced him up. "He won't negotiate with you. He doesn't care about me that much."

I cracked my neck as I surveyed the woods around us. This time the magic came to me full force. The brightness of the interwebs of magic almost brought me to my knees. I pressed my hand to my chest as I narrowed my eyes to get a better view. We were completely surrounded. "We are here for Damian. We have something that he might want back."

A woman stepped from the woods, her onyx skin glistened in the moonlight. "What could we possibly want with him? He's probably given up all of our information."

Micah spat at Mav. I expected the big brute to lose his cool on that one. He simply smiled as the salvia rolled down his cheek then splattered against his shoulder. "Damian spelled us against torture. You know that."

A man walked out of the woods behind the woman to look at Micah with weary eyes. "He doesn't look like he's working with them. You know what a shit actor he was, especially when we would go scouting for new wolves."

For good measure, Mav grinned as he punched Micah in the stomach. The poor man fell to the ground and Mav didn't stop there. He continued to kick the poor man while he was down.

The woman held her hand up. "Stop, Damian will want to see him."

Knox leaned against my car as Archer marched forward. "You won't get him back until we see Jade."

There was a snicker from the trees. "You won't be seeing Jade. She isn't taking visitors at the moment." His voice made my stomach drop. They were hurting her. "But we will be happy to make a trade with you." The man that came out of the woods had long blond hair that brushed past his shoulders. He wore fighting leathers similar to ours and based on the golden threads pulsing around him, he had a lot of magic at his disposal. When his eyes landed on mine, his brows furrowed with confusion.

"What do you have in mind?" Knox watched him with a bored expression.

"Jade told you that she didn't need rescuing, why would you come back for her? She is perfectly happy here." The man didn't look at me again as he spoke to the men. Good, I hoped he underestimated me. I was going to rip his heart out first.

Archer shrugged. "You're right, we miss Jade, but there are bigger fish to fry here. The King of the Rogues for starters. We would like to meet him."

The man grinned. "There it is. You sense power here."

I rolled my eyes. How insufferable. Power-hungry men were the worst. The big bad witch rolled his eyes back to me. "I would love to *dissect* the magic inside of you."

A growl ripped through the air and shook the ground beneath my feet. Knox stalked toward the man. "You will not look at her again."

## CHAPTER 49
TRACEY

The estate was hidden with magic. As soon as we passed through the trees, we were walking on a concrete driveway to a massive modern-looking castle. Behind it was a rubble pile that had once been the residence of all the witches and wolves Damian had under his thumb. Now it looked like it was ancient ruins. Barely anything was left of it.

The man must have sensed power inside of Knox because he didn't look in my direction again, either that or he didn't want to poke the bear. I couldn't ignore how hot the possessiveness was, but on another note… It was extremely annoying. But everything Knox did got on my nerves. He was just that kind of person. He could sneeze and somehow he would make it irritating.

The man leading us flicked his fingers to the left and the oak door swung open with zero effort. No one stood on the other side. We were walking into the den of monsters and nothing worried me more. My eyes surveyed everything around us as Archer shoved our *prisoner* forward and he stumbled walking up the steps. My fingers twitched for a knife or even my claws to poke through. I didn't like this at all. Everything inside me was screaming *danger*!

The magic in the air had stilled. There didn't seem to be any magical energy around us as we continued into the keep. At the end of the long hallway, a man stood with his back toward us. He was either awfully stupid or too powerful for his own good. When he turned around his magical aura blinded me momentarily. How could he even see? He had to be able to see through the walls with that much magic.

I inhaled deeply through my nose and the magic settled a bit but not enough for me to get a good read on him. What I wouldn't give for Granny to be here. Archer shoved Micah forward and he scrambled across the floor. My lip lifted in a sneer.

"Disgusting," I whispered as I crossed my arms over my chest.

"The Crimson Clan," the witch grinned. "Yes,

it's finally nice to meet all of you." His hair was brushed back away from his face and there were little spots of red on his hands and shirt. My stomach clenched. *No.*

Knox cocked his head. "Crimson *Pack*."

His grin only grew. "Yes, my apologies. I'm Damian."

I swallowed hard but at least he didn't look at me. Mav took a step forward. "By order of the Pack Law, you must stop creating and harboring wolves against their will."

"You're the enforcers of the Pack Law now?" Damian's grin stayed in place. He was a handsome bastard but I could see the cruel calculating look in his eyes.

Knox cracked his knuckles. "No, not entirely. But we will be someday."

Damian jutted his head forward while he sucked on his teeth. All that mattered was that we got Micah in. We needed to get out sooner rather than later. "I don't answer to Pack Law, but my plans are to abolish it."

Archer took a deep breath as he leaned against the wall. "Is Jade okay?"

Damian's eyes remained on Knox. "Yes, she is currently dining with my five-star chef." His words smelled like truth but there was something else. He wasn't being completely truthful. Archer took a step forward and a growl rumbled through the area.

Damian shook his head. "You came into my home, you try to negotiate with one of the men you kidnapped and you expect me to care about what you want or don't want?"

"We only miss our friend," I whispered. It was true. I desperately missed her and all I wanted to do was get her out of here. That was all that mattered. I didn't care if he wanted to rule the world, we could stop that later.

Damian's eyes roved over my body. It took every ounce of willpower to keep my eyes lowered to the ground while he did it. I had to look submissive. "The witch and the wolf. All wrapped up and delivered right to me. What is better than that? You're even prettier than Jade."

Knox growled again but this time it wasn't as threatening. We were in the belly of the beast. He would be stupid to provoke a powerful witch in his own domain, with even more powerful monsters lurking around where we couldn't see.

Damian smirked. "Yes, and you're powerful." He inhaled and I finally looked up at him. His face held wonder as he closed his eyes to savor the scent.

"I do love a challenge. I might just let the witches after you. They love half breeds even more than I do."

*Lie.*

He snapped his fingers and a man marched from a doorway to the left. He scooped Micah off of the floor. "Take him to the *infirmary*." The way he said it made me believe he was bringing Micah somewhere else. "As for all of you, I hate to say it but whatever you hoped to accomplish today, it won't be happening. I have lots of things to plan, starting with the downfall of your Alpha."

My jaw ticked.

"How about this?" Damian watched as Micah was half-dragged down the hall. "I know you have the children and I know you aren't here just for a simple talk. I'll let you go but only so you can tell your Alpha what's coming for him."

## CHAPTER 50
JADE

"You need to eat," the man said from the doorway. His hands shook as he pushed a tray into the cell I had been forced into. I had fought and scratched but it was no use. My body was too weak to escape the prison I had been thrown in. I kicked the tray away with my bare foot and slid back into the dark corner. Starving myself was better than eating the wolfsbane in the food. I shook my head hard and it felt like the room was spinning. He exhaled hard. "You don't understand, he said you will eat or I will be punished. My family will be punished."

I didn't want to see the poor man's family punished but I also wasn't going to be weak in here. Whatever Damian had done to my skin, it was a sickly color and I had a feeling I was running a fever. Every few seconds I either felt like I was on fire or ice cold. I shook my head again. There was nothing I could do to help this man. He had to help himself. If they all rose up, they could have more power than Damian. They could liberate themselves but there was nothing I could do while I withered away in the darkness.

There was a shout before a door slammed down the hall. It rattled the bars on the door to my cell. I didn't worry about getting my hopes up on anything exciting happening. Damian was probably in another mood and coming to take it out on me. I curled my arms around my knees and rested my chin on the tops of them. As the shouting grew closer, my hands began to shake.

I would fight. I would try. I wouldn't allow him to hurt me again.

My fingers balled into fists as I prepared for him to try to hurt me again. My body trembled as I tensed. Except, it wasn't Damian that came flying through the door. It was Micah with a guard behind him. My shoulders straightened as I pushed out of the corner. The guard tossed him into the cell with me. He tumbled across the cobblestones and came to a skidding stop at my feet. His face looked like it had been beaten into a pulp.

The chef that had delivered my food had disappeared. The door to our cell slammed closed. Micah rose off of the floor in a jerky fashion.

"What are you doing?" he croaked out as the guard went to turn to leave.

The guard didn't turn back to us but threw over his shoulder. "You aren't one of us. You are probably the reason Damian is insane right now."

"Did Damian tell you to do this?" Micah yelled. The guard didn't answer and we were left alone. Micah wasted no time. He whipped around faster than an injured man should have. He knelt down beside me and took my hands in his. "It's time to go, little wolf."

I reared back. "What?"

Micah shook his head as he surveyed the walls and pulled me to my feet. "We don't have much time, Jade. You need to get up."

My body shook as I was forced to my feet. Pain laced straight through my stomach and it took every ounce of my power not to double over on the injury causing me so much pain. I sucked air through my teeth and managed to stand up straight.

"We can't get out of here." I shook my head. There was no way out.

Micah rolled his eyes. "They've drugged you

enough they don't have any cameras down here. There is only one line of electricity running through this dungeon. It isn't enough for cameras and lights. All the guards are worried about the threat above us, currently."

I frowned as I followed him to the door. He closed his eyes, took a deep breath, and yanked on the iron. It didn't protest as he pulled it free from the wall. He was careful to place the massive door on the ground and leaned it against the wall. It hardly made a sound.

"The wolves will be listening, we have to be careful." He tucked my hand inside of his. "Are you okay to run?"

His eyes dipped to my stomach. My eyebrows pulled together. "What do you know?"

"Did he carve a 'D' into your stomach?"

I pulled my hand out of his and took a step away from him. "What's going on?"

"That's for Rafe to explain. He felt your pain and the same thing happened to him."

I gasped. "Damian must have used magic. He wanted you all to come out and find me. This is a trap."

Micah put his hands on either of my shoulders. "Damian is preoccupied above us. That is all that matters. We have to get you out. There are tunnels down here. Thank goodness I didn't have to try to find you. Damian made all of this easier for me."

I held my hand up. "What about the children?"

Micah grinned. "They're safe. We got them out. He kept all of his eggs in one basket."

"Tunnels?"

Micah nodded. "Yes, there are tunnels down here. I went over the blueprints of the house months ago. I didn't know if I would need a way to escape. Thankfully I did that or this would be going a lot worse right now."

It couldn't be that easy and I refused to believe anything otherwise. Until we got to my pack, I wouldn't feel safe. I wouldn't feel like I won. I didn't know if that would be enough. Damian was more powerful than we knew and he was holding it all back. He would find me again. I pressed my back against the wall and refused to go on.

"He will find me again, I can't leave."

Micah's face fell. "He will not get to you again, do you understand me?"

I couldn't look him in the eye. He had think I was so weak. He had to think I wasn't a wolf anymore. What kind of wolf felt this way? Not a brave one, not a good one. I wrapped my arms around myself and turned back toward the cell. Micah could get out and I would stay. It was what had to happen. I had to protect my friends.

"Listen to me, if I come out of here without you, I will not make the trip back to the Pack Lands. Do you understand me? Rafe will murder me himself. He entrusted me with this." He lifted my chin with his finger. "He entrusted me with *you*. You are all that matters right now. We aren't afraid of Damian. We will cross that bridge when we get there. Right now, your friends are putting their lives in danger above us so I can get you free."

A realization smacked me in the face. "Lucas is still up there." I turned toward the stairs that led up to the chaos.

Micah shook his head. "Definitely not. You are the only one that matters. Do you hear me?"

I gulped. "I don't care. If we don't get Lucas, I don't go with you. He put his life in danger as much as all of you have. He is probably worried sick about me."

Micah clenched his jaw as he considered. "You're really going to be stubborn about this?"

I crossed my arms over my chest and ignored the pain running through my body. I could get through this. We could get through this. I just had to be a little stronger for a little longer. "I will die on this hill."

Micah sighed before he shook his head. "If this entire operation goes down the toilet, I'm going to make sure Rafe knows it was you that botched this job."

I shrugged. "So be it."

## CHAPTER 51
JADE

The steps were a different kind of torture. My body screamed in protest with every single step. Somehow I managed to swallow back my sobs as we took them one at a time. Based on Micah's wolf hearing, there were no wolves at the door. There was a commotion on the other side of the property. It sounded like a fight but he couldn't be sure. It was enough of a distraction. We took a left at the top of the stairs and went straight for the rooms. My head spun but somehow I managed to stay upright. Micah kept his fingers on my elbow to keep me steady.

The hallways were quiet but there was surveillance in this part of the estate. If we weren't careful everything would go wrong very fast. Micah said we had to look like he was escorting me back to my room. It was the best and only plan we had.

When he opened the door and shoved me through. Lucas immediately jumped on him. He hit him over the head with the chair leg and Micah sprawled to the floor. My vision swam and I took a dive sideways.

"Shit," Micah grumbled from the floor. "I knew it was a mistake to come back for him."

Lucas grumbled something under his breath while he picked me up from the floor. The pain was too intense in my stomach to think of anything else. The room around me was a blur.

"We came back for you before Micah broke me out," my voice came out in a slurred mess. I pressed my hand against my stomach and I watched in horror as I realized it was soaked through and my hand came back red.

Micah swore again. "I didn't know it was still fresh. He must have used wolfsbane to cut her open."

Before I knew what was happening, I was being scooped up into someone's arms and my eyes shuttered closed. "Don't leave Lucas behind." I breathed before it all went dark.

. . .

The pain in my stomach was what brought me back to consciousness. I didn't know how much time had passed but I did know whoever was carrying was running for their life. There were shouts and growls then an explosion behind us. My head hustled this way and that. With all the movement I couldn't make out what was going on and I didn't have enough control over my body to hold my head still throughout it all.

"What's happening?" I didn't know if the words even passed my lips until Lucas looked down at me. He was the only thing I could focus on. His face was pained and his teeth were gritted together.

"Damian isn't very happy about us taking his property." Lucas grimaced.

"Where's Micah?" I didn't know how I was even speaking legibly.

"He's holding them off for us," Lucas squeezed his eyes closed as his body jerked like he had been hit.

"I can walk."

He tightened his hold on me. "Like hell you can, your wounds are weeping blood and you smell sick. If you don't let me get you out of here, all of this will be for nothing. We are not dying today, Jade."

I could see it on his face that each step hurt him but he continued anyway. There was another explosion behind us and Lucas grinned. "I think our pack is excited."

I closed my eyes again but this time I listened to all the commotion around us. My wolf instincts and abilities weren't back to full force but I was trying. The commotion was deafening. There were pops and cracks of wolves transforming, electricity crackling in the distance, and subtle cries and grunts of pain.

"I have only transformed once, but I don't know what else to do." My eyes snapped open. There was no way Lucas could transform into his wolf with all the wolfsbane we had been consuming. He pressed his lips together as his eyes looked around us. We were still on Damian's property but at least we were out of the actual building.

I shook my head against his arm. "No, we won't make it if you do that."

"No one is on our trail, it will only take a minute."

Before I could protest, he was laying me on the grass and stripping his clothes off. A tear slid down my cheek as his bones cracked and popped out of place. This could very well be the last time we saw each other. I couldn't transform with him. His brown eyes locked onto mine. "You're going to have to get onto my back as soon as I am a wolf. Do not hesitate."

I got up into a crouch, even though my body hated me for it. His face elongated into a snout as chocolate fur rippled and rolled over his skin. He fell forward onto his hands and knees before a howl ripped from his lips. Right before his tail extended from his backend, I jumped onto his back. I threaded my fingers through the fur at the base of his neck and he jumped forward. Agony shot through my middle but I didn't ease my grip on him.

Heat at my back made worry course through my body but I didn't pay it any mind and neither did Lucas. Was Micah back there? Was he going to make it out okay? I squeezed my eyes closed and pressed my face into Lucas's furry back. He smelled like a new kind of home to me. Like pine needles and hot cocoa. Like safety and love. A different kind of love I had never experienced before. Tears pricked at my eyes again but I pushed them back. I had to keep a level head throughout all of this. We couldn't afford my emotions right now. All that mattered was getting to safety then I could fall apart afterwards.

The wind whipped my hair away from my face and shoulders as we zoomed forward. Lucas's heart raced beneath my hands. His rapid breathing matched my own. Sweat slid down my temples as he leapt into the sky then landed hard. I could barely feel the pain in my stomach as I felt my consciousness slip again. I blinked my eyes rapidly to stay awake. Lucas growled and I was abruptly brought back to reality. He must have sensed me slipping again.

I rubbed my fingers back and forth in his fur to let him know I was still awake. His responding purr sent a wave of comfort through me. When he came to a halt, I picked my head up from the warmth of his body. Two wolves were waiting for us on the other side of the path. One had a gray streak through his black fur and the other was pure white with a black spot over its eyes. They growled together before they slinked forward. I went to slide off of Lucas's back when he bucked me back on. We would do this together. I swallowed hard as the wolves circled us. Their heads were low to the ground while their fur on the back of their neck stood up in the air. This wasn't good.

The scent of my blood was still pungent. I couldn't fight with Lucas or I would die out here. I couldn't risk it with the wolfsbane keeping Nalia down. My fingers sunk deeper into Lucas's fur before he pounced. The other wolf didn't see it coming and dove to the dirt. It was exactly what Lucas had wanted him to do. We soared over the black wolf. Lucas didn't let up his pace as we continue to run. How much farther? My stomach clenched with a dull ache and I knew I didn't have much time. Would I actually live through this? Was it all for nothing?

Lucas tossed his head over his shoulder to look at me but his eyes didn't meet mine. They looked at something beyond me. A howl split the air and I turned around just in time to see Micah covered in wolves while he transformed back into his human form. He continued to slash with his claw extended hands but it meant nothing when one of them wrapped his teeth around Micah's neck. His shoulders slumped as he fell to the ground and my heart went down with him. His eyes glistened with tears as he saluted us before the wolves completely covered him from our sight.

## CHAPTER 52
RAFE

Ford stood next to me on the steps to the Crimson Manor. His stance mirrored my own. His face probably showed more emotion than mine did, but for some reason, I knew it was because he was more worried than I was.

My brother didn't know my Guardians like I did. He didn't know their fighting routine or how serious they could be when it mattered. They knew what to do when the going got tough. I trusted no one more with my mate's safety.

Tracey would die before she let anything happen to her friend. I squeezed my eyes closed as the minutes ticked by. I felt useless. I was more than useless but I had promised I would stay behind so they didn't have to worry about me too. After all, it was a trap. I couldn't get caught up in that. My pack needed me. My mate would need me. My family needed me. I couldn't do anything rash even though everything inside of me was screaming to go there and rescue her myself.

Ford touched my arm gently. "Don't worry, they'll bring her back."

The scent of steaks cooking inside made me nauseated. Usually, I could tear up a kitchen right now when I was anxious like this but there was too much at risk. We had never had a mission this important before. Yes, they were all important in their own way. We had saved children. We had liberated Granny from a toxic coven. We had done so much good, but this was different and I hated every second I had to wait. I couldn't even check in on them.

I shoved off of the front steps and paced across the worn dirt path. "At that rate, you're going to have a tunnel to China." My mother's voice usually brought me comfort and peace but not today. I didn't listen to her as I walked back and forth. I rubbed the back of my neck as I watched the drive. It was too late to be up and really past Ford's bedtime. He liked to complain and object to having one, but he was still a grouch without sufficient sleep. He did well on pack nights but not if his wolf didn't get a good run in.

"There's no point in waiting out here," my mother's voice trembled. "You're going to get sick." I loved that she tried to be the traditional mother to me even though our bodies could withstand frigid temperatures. "You're going to get heartsick."

This time I looked up and the expression on her face almost brought me to my knees. All of her pain from losing her mate was right there in her eyes. All of that pain was because of me. My wolf perked up in my head and whined. He was usually the vicious side of me. He fought first and asked questions later. He was the reason I had a pair of Jade's panties shoved in the bottom of my sock drawer. He was the irrational one who liked to hunt our prey and our mate. But today, he felt remorse over what we had to do for our pack. He felt just as terrible as I did.

So I climbed the worn steps and wrapped my arms around her shoulders. I pressed a quick kiss to her forehead and blinked back the growing moisture in my eyes. Maybe this time I could put it all aside for someone else. Someone that had absolutely nothing to gain from my pain. She sighed contently before she patted my back. "You remind me of him every day."

I knew she meant before he got sick but a little voice in the back of my head reminded me that if I got sick, I would have to be put down too. If something happened to Jade, I wouldn't be far off from where my father left off.

I had managed to wolf down most of my steak when the sound of tires on gravel had me flying out of my chair. Ford and my mother were right on my heels. The rest of the pack was sound asleep. I imagined Granny was still awake, I didn't think she ever slept, but she was nowhere to be found. She would come out when she was ready. She would assist when needed but she had little minds to tend to.

Tracey's car was the first one in the drive. Behind her was Mav on his motorcycle and Archer's SUV. No other motorcycle pulled forward. I rushed to the side of Tracey's vehicle and pulled the door. The way it groaned I imagined it flying through the sky. I didn't care one bit what happened to this car. I could scent my mate and rot in the air. She was all that mattered. My wolf came up to the forefront in my head. His grumble vibrated my chest. He was ready to fight for our mate.

*No need, bud.* She's in good hands now.

The seats in the back of Tracey's car had been ripped out and the floor had been assembled in a makeshift bed. A wolf that hardly fit in the car was nuzzled around her head like a lap cat. I ignored the unfamiliar wolf if he was civil in the car. Most wolves couldn't stand being in their wolf form in such a small space. I didn't know how the massive oaf survived it. Until I really looked down at my mate.

The world around us faded. Everything was happening so fast but through my head, it was in slow motion. Jade's shirt was gone and all that covered her chest was a thin strip of fabric. A little pair of shorts was stretched over her backside. Deep cuts marked up and down her legs in a grotesque fashion. But the worst of it was the deep, jagged 'D' in the center of her stomach. Blood and infection poured from the wound. I reached forward but someone slapped me away.

It took a moment for the sounds to rush back to me. The wolf by Jade's head was growling. Tracey was screaming something about needing Granny. Knox was being carried from Archer's backseat and my mother was shouting orders to the rest of the pack as they emerged from their homes to see what all the fuss was about.

"Bring her to my home," my words halted everything else. "I have a room for her there."

It wasn't much but it was quiet and away from the prying eyes of the pack members. Tracey got back in the car as I ordered Archer to do the same. Knox would be brought back to my house too. It was the best I could do. The infirmary had been prepared for whatever outcome but I couldn't allow them to go there. I couldn't stomach it. My wolf ripped through my skin. The trees flashed by as I outran their vehicles. I managed to make it to my house before them and pulled my clothes out from the wooden steps. My dad had designed the house like that. All around the porch there were little airtight compartments to keep clothes and shoes in case a shift came on unexpectedly. I shoved my legs into a pair of loose-fitting boxers as Archer's car skidded forward. This time Knox pushed the door open and collapsed beside it. Mav was next to him in a matter of seconds.

I pointed to the front of the house that had been left unlocked. "First door, down the hall, on the left. There's a twin bed in there and bandages in the nightstand."

Knox grinned at me as the boys helped him up the steps. "You missed a good fight, buddy."

"Next time I'll fight by your side," I pressed my hand into his shoulder as they passed. Blood spotted his naked skin but I couldn't tell if it was fresh or not. It smelled like his but he seemed to be healing alright as he walked up the stairs. Tracey's car took a few seconds to slide beside Archer's. Her face was grim and there was blood splattered on her fighting leathers. From what I could see and smell, she wasn't injured but she had done a lot of killing. The scent of death clung to her skin.

The same wolf stayed curled up at my mate's side. I looked at Tracey as I bent forward and tried to think of the best way to retrieve my mate. Mav was back beside me in no time. His big bushy brows were pulled together on his forehead and sweat slid down his temples. "What do we do?"

"I'm going to hand her to you," I whispered as I climbed into the backseat carefully. He nodded before he stood up straight. A yell made the hairs on the back of my arms stand up.

Mav pressed his lips together with a grim expression. "He was shot with bullets laced with wolfsbane. Knox will be fine, but having to cut through his skin to get them out won't be fun. For any of us."

I nodded my head once then began to scoot my mate's body from the car. Tracey watched beside Mav with a pale face. One of her hands was pressed to her lips. I didn't know how I managed it but after a few painstaking minutes, I had Jade in Mav's arms. As soon as I was free from the tiny backseat and the wolf hopped out, Mav gave Jade back to me immediately.

It was like muscle memory from the night she had curled herself around me after that painful shift. She winced as we climbed the steps and I wondered the kind of person and wolf she would be after all of this.

My wolf whined in my head but somehow it escaped outside my body. A howl itched at the back of my throat. All I wanted to do was fix her immediately but even if it was possible for her body, it wouldn't be for her mind.

## CHAPTER 53
RAFE

Granny had managed to get most of the wolfsbane out of Jade's system with an IV and a little magical help. Granny had been a nurse in another life before she met Tracey's grandfather. She had saved lives with her magical knowledge and her medical skills. When we were little we would sit around in her cottage to listen to all the stories of all the lifetimes she had lived. She especially loved being a nurse in the Second World War. She had hated the destruction, but she had loved how many she had saved and helped. She didn't mind being on the frontlines if it meant saving people. She had left in the dead of the night when Jade's vitals had evened out.

Granny had told me to get some rest, but just

like Tracey and the mysterious wolf, we wouldn't be leaving her side any time soon. Tracey yawned on the couch across the room and the wolf shifted away from her. He slept on the floor and his chocolate-colored fur would ruffle every time Tracey moved.

"Who's the wolf?" I finally asked as the sun took a peek through the windows. Jade still hadn't woken but her skin didn't look so green anymore and the scent of infection didn't linger in the air.

Tracey shrugged as she eyed him suspiciously. He smelled familiar but I couldn't place it. It probably had something to do with my mate's scent covering him from head to toe, but I chose to ignore that for now. There would be a lot of questions when and if he decided to transform back into his human form. Though, he looked rather content to keep his identity a secret. "He won't leave her side and he won't shift back."

I ran my tongue over my teeth. "I thought Micah said no one was coming back with them."

Tracey ground her teeth together. "He did. He was very adamant on that."

"What happened then?" I leaned back in my chair as I watched the wolf. His brown eyes never left Jade and my eyes didn't leave him. I didn't like how much he smelled like my mate and how much she smelled like him. But if she had found a friend in there that had helped her escape all of the pain, then could I really be that mad?

Tracey leaned her elbows on her knees. "We ran into a hiccup with Damian, he didn't want us to leave without a fight. He wanted to relay a message back to you. He knows we were the ones that freed the children. His witches came at us full force and honestly, I don't know how we even got out of there." Her eyes went distant. "It was bad. Knox was shot first then wolves poured into the hallway. One minute we were there and the next we were out in the middle of the yard."

My brows furrowed. "Did you use magic?"

She shrugged her shoulders up to her blood-splattered ears. "I have no idea. I don't know what the hell happened. Then we were running for our lives and wolves continued to pour out from the woods. He has an army bigger than I have ever seen before." She gulped. "If the witches don't get out of there, then we are done for. Granny and I can't hold off those numbers. We need help from Pack Law."

It was the last thing I wanted to do but if Tracey's account checked out with the rest of the men, then she was right. We wouldn't be able to do this on our own. But why did this Damian character want to do this at all?

"How did you get to Jade?"

Tracey tucked her chin against her chest. "We literally ran into each other. Micah was nowhere to be seen. There were wolves everywhere and then there was this wolf," she nodded her head at the stranger. "With freaking Jade on his back running like I had never seen before. It was something from a movie, I swear."

"Why didn't you transform?" The details were the only thing keeping me sane.

"Someone had to drive," She grinned with triumph. "I knew that our cars would be our only hope. The other boys had already thrown themselves into their wolf forms. I really didn't have much of a choice then I saw Jade slipping from consciousness. She couldn't hold onto the wolf's back anymore. I had to carry her the rest of the way while the boys fought off what they could."

I nodded my appreciation. "Go take a shower, get some food in you then check on the rest of the Guardians."

She went to object. I held my hand up. "I will not leave my mate's side, especially when we have a stranger wolf that won't leave even though he doesn't seem to pose a threat. I need the men checked on and you're one of the only ones I trust to do it right. See if they need anything from Granny while you're at it."

Tracey nodded before she disappeared. I looked at the wolf curled up in the corner. "I know you aren't going to speak back to me, and that's perfectly okay. But here are some ground rules." He perked up his head. "You will not harm my mate. If you do, I will rip your throat out before asking Jade if it's okay. I do owe you a life debt for saving my mate's life but I'm not sure if I want to offer it to you just yet." He dipped his head in understanding. "Thank you for getting her out or helping her get far enough for my people to help her. Until we know who you are, you aren't permitted around the people here. You will not leave my home. This place is under constant surveillance too. Don't try any funny business."

He nodded his head again before he laid it on his front paws and his eyes went back to watching my mate.

## CHAPTER 54
JADE

There was a thick coating on my tongue when my consciousness returned to me. My lips smacked together for a brief moment before I tried to sit up.

"Don't try to be strong, you can remain resting," Granny's voice wrapped around me in a warm embrace. I opened my eyes to come face to face with her. She smiled warmly and tears sprang from my eyes. She dabbed at my face with a tissue that materialized out of thin air. "None of that. You must reserve your strength for healing your body. You still have large amounts of wolfsbane in your system and your body was cut open with a blade dipped in it."

I leaned back into the fluffy pillows at my back. The room I was in was beautiful. The walls were a white shiplap and the bed I laid in was a massive four-poster that was distressed with ivory. Dark brown peaked out from beneath the paint in small slashes. In front of the windows was a light grey couch and a glass coffee table in front of it. Across from that was a recliner that looked out of place with its worn leather. Where was I?

Next to the couch was a familiar chocolate wolf. "You still haven't transformed back?"

Granny followed my gaze to the wolf that looked more like an overgrown puppy. "He refuses to leave your side."

"How long have I been asleep?" My stomach was still tender beneath the massive white bandages around my middle.

"Four days," She pressed his lips together in a grim line. "Your body needed the rest."

I couldn't wrap my head around that time frame and the fact that Lucas still hadn't left the room. How was he still alive?

"You can go relieve yourself or something," I snickered as his ears lifted from his head. "I'm sure you have to go like something bad."

He let out a wolfish laugh before he bounced up and out of the room. I doubted he would stay gone for long.

Granny checked my pulse before she leaned forward and pressed her ear against my chest. "You sound better than you have in days. Do you want to try to walk?"

I nodded my head and she gave me her hand for support. I could do this. My knees wobbled before I put any weight on them. Granny's fingers grasped mine in a hard grip. My weight shifted as I leaned forward.

The bedroom door opened. Instead of standing up on weak legs, my head snapped in the opposite direction. Rafe stood in the doorway with a tray of food in his hands. Granny let go of my fingers and shot me a timid smile. "I will leave you to it, I'll come back in a few hours to change your bandages and make sure everything is still healing properly."

I didn't take my eyes off of the man standing in the doorway as Granny ambled around him. He wore a black v-neck t-shirt that seemed to be a little too small and his jeans were worn at the knees but there were no holes. It was odd to see him without shoes on, only wearing black socks. His hair was even longer than it had been last time. It was tied back at the nape of his neck with a ponytail holder.

My fingers curled into fists as I had the unnatural urge to pull the band free and run my finger through it. I wondered if his hair was as soft as it looked.

I closed my eyes briefly as I mentally reprimanded myself. His voice was rough in the empty bedroom. It didn't belong in the white open space. "I didn't think you would be awake yet."

I could have tried to stand on my own, except I didn't want Rafe to see me weak. I didn't want him to see me fall. "That smells good."

He climbed up on the other side of the bed with ease. The orange juice in the clear glass cup sloshed sideways but didn't escape onto the tray. On the plate in the center of it was toast, waffles, different kinds of fruit, and a hefty pile of bacon. My stomach grumbled in approval. He sat the tray across my lap, careful for my stomach, and leaned back into the pillows on the other side. He looked so comfortable and at ease.

The bacon was cooked to perfection as I bit into it. Not too much crunch but not undercooked. A flashback had me choking on the bite. The inside of the cafeteria when I wondered when was the last time I had enjoyed food. I washed it down with the OJ while I ignored Rafe's questioning gaze.

"Where's-" I cut myself off before I said Lucas's

name. I couldn't give his identity away until he was ready. "Where's my friend?"

"He's eating breakfast downstairs like a dog." Rafe's lips turned down in disgust. "He won't change back."

I knew it had something to do with how scared he was of what they would think of him. He had been gone for so long. *Five years.* What would they think of him now? I hummed in the back of my throat while I avoided the bacon and ate everything else on the tray.

"He smells like you," His voice was soft, softer than it had ever been. Why was he here? Didn't he have Alpha things to do?

I nodded my head. "We have been together since Damian kidnapped me."

"Together?" He cleared his throat and rubbed the back of his neck.

"Yes, we shared a room. He's been my best friend this whole time. I don't know what I would have done without him."

Before I knew what was happening, Rafe brushed his fingers across the bare skin of my neck. I had forgotten about the bruising there. "Did he do this to you?"

I snorted before I pulled away from his touch.

"No, he would never. He cares about me a lot more than many others do." Rafe nodded his head like he could understand. "Where's my phone?"

He frowned. "When you got here, they had stripped most of your clothes from you. They needed to see the extent of your wounds."

My phone was gone, which meant that Damian could get to my parents. Before I could mentally prepare myself, I launched myself from the bed and about face-planted. Rafe had his arms braced around me carefully, keeping me from hitting the floor. "Where are you going?"

"My parents," I gasped out against the pain in my middle. "They're going to be targeted by Damian next if I don't protect them."

His smile about broke my heart. "You aren't going to be protecting anyone in this state. Gabriel is posted at their home and we have some reinforced magic helping, as well. Good thing they moved so close to our property."

My hands clenched his biceps against my better judgment. His gaze darted down to my lips and somehow I managed to scramble from his grip without hitting the floor. I crossed my feet beneath me and scowled up at him. "I need to do this on my own."

He held his hands up in surrender. "Of course."

Lucas came bounding through the door a few minutes later, right on time to rescue me.

Lucas and I were sitting beneath the trees outside when I finally brought it up. "You have to tell them who you are."

He didn't say anything and instead tucked his head into my lap. I ran my fingers through the fur at the base of his skull and felt a wave of contentment wash through me. If only every day could feel like that. He had helped me down the stairs and out the house that I had later discovered was Rafe's home. For whatever reason, I had thought he lived at the main house. His home sat beautiful and bright in the distance from where we sat with our picnic. The basket was full of fruits and vegetables. I was thankful for the array. I didn't know if I could stomach meat anytime soon.

"I know you're scared, but you have to know that they miss and love you so much. I know my family would want me back no matter what."

He picked his head up and I could practically read his expression. *Then you tell your parents what you are.*

I rolled my eyes. "It isn't as easy. Your family is supernatural already. Plus Tracey is a witch now. Weirder things have probably happened."

This time he rolled his brown eyes.

"I'll be with you every step of the way but they aren't going to continue to let you stay here if they don't know who you are. They're going to think you're a threat. I would rather them know you."

He sighed and laid his head back down. My eyes sought out the windows on Rafe's home and for a moment, I swore I saw the curtains flutter and a man disappearing from sight.

## CHAPTER 55
JADE

It took Tracey longer than I expected to come find me. As soon as Lucas saw her or scented her approach, he was up and gone. He couldn't stand to be near her for too long. I wondered if it was because he was desperate for her approval and knew he couldn't get it yet.

She sat down across from me. Her wiry curls were somewhat tamed in a braid down her back. Her skin was scrubbed clean and she actually wore a pink long sleeve top with black pants. I didn't think I had ever seen her in pink before. It complimented her skin tone nicely.

I grinned at her. "Aren't you a sight for sore eyes?"

A little smile materialized onto her face. "I missed you."

I leaned over to pull her into my arms for a hug. Her hand brushed my stomach and I winced. She pulled out of my embrace and worry took over her features. "Do you need anything? I'm so sorry!"

I held my hands up. "I'm fine, it was only a little pain."

Tracey looked around us in panic.

"Don't be like that." My voice broke.

Her brows pulled together. "Like what?"

"Like I'm going to break at any moment."

She shook her head. "You just might."

"I promise you, I've been through worse."

She didn't look so convinced.

"Okay, maybe not," I shrugged. "But I will get better and when I do, I'll be stronger for it."

Her eyes wouldn't meet mine. "All of this is my fault."

"Is that why you won't look at me?"

My friend didn't answer but instead watched the woods. "Who is the wolf?"

I let out a groan. "Don't go about changing the subject on me."

She leaned back onto her hands. "It's bothering me too. All of this is bothering me. I have never felt so out of control in my entire life and I just need things to start making sense again."

I scooted closer to her and picked up her hands in mine. They were scarred and callused. "None of this is your fault. They would have come after me at any time. They are the ones to blame. Okay? Damian is. Not you. Never any of you. Could we have all done better? Absolutely but I know without a shadow of a doubt that we are stronger now. We will be better now."

A tear streaked down her cheek. "I just wish none of this had happened."

Tears threatened my eyes. "Me too, but its okay. I value my pack a lot more than I did before."

Tracey perked up. "Your pack?"

I smiled. "I guess I need to tell the alpha-hole that, huh?"

Tracey snickered. "I'm sure he will be thrilled."

"Let's not hold our breath. I'm sure he's still the asshole he was before I was kidnapped."

Rafe wasn't at his home when we finally got up to go inside hours later. The fresh air and sunlight did me wonders and I didn't want to go inside. But eventually, both of our stomachs grumbled and there wasn't anything left in the picnic basket.

There also wasn't any food in Rafe's brand new fridge either. When we got in Tracey's car, Lucas hopped right into the trunk. All Tracey did was frown.

"My friend has been with me since the beginning, I love him more than I think I've ever loved a friend." Hurt flashed across Tracey's face at my words. "He was there for me in a time and place that no one should have to be. I love him in a different way but that doesn't mean I love you any less."

Tracey looked at him in the rearview mirror. "There's just something about him that I can't quite put my finger on. The webs of magic around him tell a story that I can't decipher. Did you bring home another hybrid?"

I changed the subject instead. "Did you check on Knox?"

Tracey gave me side-eyes. "Yes, he's recovering at the training grounds."

"I have a feeling this land is a lot bigger than what I think it is."

Tracey laughed and the sound made me feel whole again. It made me feel like the last few months hadn't happened. A few flurries hit the windshield and I gasped as snow fell from the sky. Children flooded the woods and the manor as we pulled up. Everywhere I looked there was magic happening. The children rushed to Tracey's car as we pulled up. Lucas flattened his ears to his head in nervousness.

The trunk opened up but all he did was try to make himself smaller against the backseat that had been put back into the car. "You're the one that decided to come with."

He shook his head once. Tracey giggled as she went to close the trunk. At last second, Lucas changed his mind and barreled into her. She fell onto her ass, laughing, as he ran right for the woods.

"Who knew kids could be so scary?" Tracey giggled again. My eyes snagged on something behind the manor. I tried to step around Tracey but she blocked my path.

"I need to see something," I said as I tried once again to get a better look at the cottage I would eventually call my home again. That is, if I still had a job. I had disappeared for a long time.

Tracey blocked me again. "I think we need to get inside to get some food."

I rolled my eyes. "I think I need to see my future home. I know it had a lot of work that needed to be finished on it before everything happened. Maybe it'll help me keep my mind off of what happened."

Guilt flashed across Tracey's face. "I have a confession."

Panic bloomed inside of my chest. What was she going to confess? "Yes?"

"I used your cottage to get myself out of the depressed state I was in. I used it to keep my mind off of the guilt I was feeling and the intense heartache. I didn't know what else to do."

A new emotion took over my body. I wrapped my arms around her middle. "How does it look?" Tracey was the only one that knew exactly what I wanted to do the place. If it had been anyone else, I would have been nervous.

"Wanna see it?" Tracey asked just as Rafe stepped out from the manor. He crossed his feet over each other and leaned against the massive beam on the porch. His eyes bore into me with a new intensity.

I nodded my head at my friend as I watched the man ahead of me. His expression was neutral and too hard to read. But when Ford walked out, I had a feeling I knew a little more about the Alpha-hole.

Ford's expression was satisfied but also relieved to see me. He mirrored his brother's stance on the porch and for a moment I wondered what Rafe would be like with a family. Would a family change him and the wolf inside of him?

I was so caught up in my thoughts about the Alpha that I didn't hear whatever Tracey was rambling on about. I came back to reality and smiled at my friend but I didn't miss Ford elbowing Rafe in the side out the corner of my eye. I pressed my lips together to fight a grin as Tracey led the way to her masterpiece. The front of the cottage had been painted all white but the trim on everything was a matte black. It even had black gutters. The front porch light had been left on and the white curtains in the front window were open.

Tears pricked my eyes as she unlocked the front door. I couldn't believe my eyes. Under the front window was a cute window box with white fake flowers. I rubbed my hands down my arms as I watched more snow touch down on the ground.

The first thing that caught my eye was the broken couch in the living room. I snickered. "What happened?"

The smile Tracey had been sporting fell away. "Mav and his fat ass. He thought it would be a great idea to take a running dive on a couch that has smaller legs than his arms." She huffed before she said sarcastically, "Makes complete sense to me."

Leave it to Mav to break the first thing in my home. As we walked down the hall, my wolf senses started to come back to me. Rafe's scent was everywhere. It coated everything. I could hardly focus on what Tracey had done to my space with the smell of him swirling around my head.

We stopped at my bedroom door where it was the strongest. "Did Rafe stay here?"

Tracey bit her bottom lip. "Yes."

I frowned. "Why?"

"He was in the process of remodeling his own home and didn't have any other place to stay. The witch kids have kind of taken over the manor at the moment."

I nodded my head. That made sense. Kind of.

Everything about my home was perfect except the missing master bath but Tracey had told me she already had blueprints drawn up for one to be added on. She wasn't allowed to continue with construction because they needed her to do other things around the pack. She had used my renovation as a crutch and the pack wasn't allowing her to do that anymore. Which was fine, because I was really itching to do something myself. It was all a dream come true but having a project to keep me busy would be a good thing. It would also be a place for my family to come and visit me, I hoped.

Rafe was sitting at the head of the table when we entered the manor. His back was straight and he was speaking low into a cellphone.

We sat down across from him and food was immediately placed in front of us. I didn't recognize the woman but Tracey smiled at her warmly so I imagined that was a good thing. Lucas was still missing but I was glad for the spare bedroom because I would be offering it to him if he didn't tell everyone who he really was. Rafe put his phone down before he popped a French fry into his mouth.

"Contractors have been called, just say the word, whenever you're ready, and they'll be here in a flash."

My mouth dropped open and Tracey snickered. "Who are you?"

"Excuse me?" Rafe put down his fry.

"You're not being an asshole."

There was a gasp from the kitchen. The corners of Rafe's lips twitched. "You have been through a lot, it's the least I can do."

"You're also his ma-" Someone said from the kitchen but before she could finish her sentence there was a loud crash followed by an even louder curse.

I looked over my shoulder but whoever had made the comment was gone. "What was she saying?"

Rafe licked his bottom lip slowly. I tried my hardest to not follow the movement, but it was rather impossible. I felt like I was in the desert and he was a tall drink of water. Water I had been missing all of my life. I blinked myself out of the daze. "There are a few things we need to discuss now that you're back. Somewhat big news."

I shook my head as I noticed Lucas out the corner of my eye. "Whatever it is, I'm sure it can wait. I have a feeling something bigger is coming."

Rafe pressed his lips together and Tracey shook her head like she couldn't believe what I was saying. I was sure there was nothing bigger than the stranger wolf identifying himself.

## CHAPTER 56
JADE

The reflection in the mirror staring back at me didn't look like myself. The scar on my stomach was very jagged and visible but at least it had healed all the way. The scars on my arms and legs weren't as bad. Granny was hopeful they would fade with time but she didn't make a comment about the one on my stomach doing so. She simply sighed as she left Rafe's home. Rafe's home that I was still staying in but I couldn't figure out why. I had my own home I could go back to, I didn't understand why I was being holed up here.

The snow continued to come down in a thick blanket outside. I shivered as I watched it float to the ground in thick fluffs. Nalia still wasn't back in my head and I wondered if she would be back anytime soon. I missed her. I missed my other half.

Rafe said I was welcome to anything in the house. I was dressed in clothes from Tracey's closet. We had trudged through the snow to get to the front porch and my poor toes were icicles. I hadn't thought to grab a few pairs of socks before I left her parents' house. They had both welcomed me with warm hugs, all while Lucas had sat outside with a sad look over his face. He wanted the acceptance they so freely gave others and I didn't blame him. I would have wanted it too if the roles were reversed.

My feet thumped on the wood floors as I walked to his massive white dresser in the closet. He had to have socks in here somewhere. I pulled open the first drawer and my shoulders sagged in relief. Socks were piled on top of each other. Black and grey fabric stared back at me from the drawer. I grabbed a pair of grey ones before my eyes snagged on something with pink lace.

I looked over my shoulder to make sure I was alone before I pulled the pink lace free. My stomach dropped and my core did something funny. It was my panties from the night of the party. My breath hitched as I shoved them back in the drawer. I turned around quickly but ran into a wall of muscle instead of the open doorway.

"Hello, little wolf, find something you like?" Rafe's eyes were bright gold now. The brown completely gone. The scent of my desire evident in the air. I had just as many issues as this Alpha-hole had.

I shook my head.

He leaned down an inch before he smirked. "Are you sure?"

I scowled up at him and crossed my arms over my chest. "Not something I liked, something rather disturbing."

"Like?" His eyes flicked over my shoulder to the open dresser drawer.

I swallowed hard before my chin went up an inch. "Like my panties from the night you forced a change on me."

"My wolf couldn't help himself. He needed you to know you were ours." Rafe's tongue glided over his top lip and my mouth went dry.

"I don't belong to anyone," I thought to the 'D' on my stomach and all desire I had felt was gone. It was replaced with something vile. Something that slithered up my throat and made me sick. I pushed past Rafe in horror and marched right to the bathroom. I would never be anyone's because Damian had marked me as his.

I slipped the socks over my feet as I sat on the side of the tub. What would intimacy be like now? Now that I had a constant reminder of my time in captivity? How would I ever feel confident again like I had before? I would never wear a bikini or crop top again. I would never feel like me.

A few minutes passed before there was a knock on the door. "I didn't mean anything by that."

"You apologize now?" My voice came out in a rough whisper, close to tears.

"If that's what it takes," He waited a second before he continued. "I'm not the best at this. Not at all but I'm trying to be better. Despite my wolf and his ancient beliefs. I want to be a good *man*. The beast is something else entirely and I can't make any promises on him."

Maybe I could meet him halfway. Maybe he wasn't as bad as I thought. Maybe everyone was right about him and that one instance shouldn't have marked everything in a bad light. I remembered what had happened when Nalia took over. I had killed twice. I had taken two lives because she had deemed it so. Was that how Rafe felt sometimes? Was that what the other wolves in the pack did?

Before I could talk myself out of it, I opened the door. I looked up at Rafe and a tear escaped my eye. It rolled down my face before it dropped onto my shoulder. "I will never be able to belong to anyone. Damian made sure of that."

Rafe's lips parted before he sighed and closed his eyes. "I wish I could take it back. That night that I felt your pain, I would have consumed it all just so you didn't feel it. I would take your scar and wear it instead of you, if I could. I would do anything to make sure that you don't feel like this anymore but I know that I can't. There is nothing I can do to change your mind. But I will say this, the scar doesn't define you or your beauty. If anything, the scar shows how strong you are. How resilient. Whether you wear it proudly someday or not, you will always be strong to me." The pad of his thumb traced the wet trail of tears on my cheek. "You are courageous. You are magnificent and I am sorry if no one has ever told you that before but I will live the rest of my days reminding you of it, whether you like me or not."

. . .

My heart clenched inside of my chest and I blinked in surprise. I didn't know what I was expecting from him, but it wasn't this. It was never this.

I opened my mouth to protest but my head didn't let me. It stopped the words before they could escape my mouth and damn us both. "I don't know what to say."

Rafe tucked a strand of hair behind my ear with his other hand. "Don't say anything. Just promise me that you will let me redeem myself?"

All I could do was nod my head.

🐾

Lucas sat next to me in bed the next day as I contemplated what we were going to do. Knox and Mav were downstairs making all sorts of racket. I needed to find Lucas some clothes for when he was ready to transform but I knew I couldn't force him into telling them anything. The only person getting frustrated with the wolf was Rafe. He would come to speak with me and there Lucas would be, sleeping in the corner. No matter how many times Rafe wanted to speak to me or be with me, we always had an audience. Rafe had been furious when he had turned around the previous night to find Lucas sitting on his haunches watching the entire exchange.

I had managed a laugh, but Rafe hardly thought it was funny. Lucas had given me his wolfish grin before he jumped onto the bed and went to sleep. I had a feeling he had been faking it for my benefit.

"You're going to have to identify yourself soon enough." Knox had brought breakfast up for us. I fed Lucas bacon while I spoke. "Rafe is allowing this but he won't be too keen on it for much longer."

Lucas rolled his brown eyes. I chewed on a bite of waffle.

"If you won't tell them, I will have to." I was pulling out the big guns now.

He sat up at that and gave me the look that said *don't you dare*.

"I'm serious," I took a sip of my orange juice. "Rafe is going to try to get the information out of me sooner rather than later. I don't know if I can resist his charms." I laughed and Lucas sighed in resignation. He tilted his head toward the bathroom. "Yes, there are clothes in there for you." He shook his head. "Do you want me to get the clothes to bring for you?" He nodded.

Finally, we were getting somewhere. I took a deep breath. "Let's do this then."

## CHAPTER 57
JADE

It was showtime. I had gathered everyone that needed to know who Lucas was in the manor. Rafe watched me with curious eyes from the head of the table but I chose to ignore him. I couldn't let his dark eyes undo me in front of everyone else. It was bad enough that I smelled like him now that I was living in his home. I had walked through the front doors to the manor and he had taken a long satisfied whiff when I walked by him. I swatted his shoulder playfully but an elated feeling had washed through me at the same time.

The Guardians all sat around the table with Tracey's family. Rafe watched me with careful eyes. I simply sat next to my best friend and waited for Lucas to make his appearance. His scent washed over the room first. Vivian leaned forward and frowned before she looked at her family. Granny's lips twitched into a knowing smile. Of course, she was aware of who the stranger wolf had been. Lucas walked around the staircase in all of his human glory. He had given himself a haircut and his face was shaved nice and clean. His clothes were a tad bulky on his frame but I knew he would fill them out now that we were out of Damian's estate.

Vivian was the first one out of her chair. It toppled backwards with a loud crack but she didn't stop until she was throwing herself into her son's arms. "Oh my gosh, oh my gosh! Is this a trick? My baby!" Her sobs shook the room as she fell apart. The next one throwing herself into the circle of emotion was Tracey. She cupped her brother's cheeks inside of her hands as her face fell.

"It's you," she whispered. "It's really you!"

Axel stood off to the side awkwardly until Tracey and Vivian untangled themselves from Lucas's arms. He stood up straighter under his father's gaze. "I can't believe it's you."

Lucas took a hesitant step toward his father and they both fell apart. Tears coated Axel's cheeks as he pulled his son into a tight embrace. Granny brushed away a few tears before she got up to hug her grandson. The emotions in the room were stifling. Everyone took turns hugging the man that had become one of my best friends.

Vivian kept her hands wrapped around her son even as everyone started to leave. I didn't imagine she would let him out of her sight for a while. "You were held captive by Damian too?"

Lucas looked down at his mother. "That's more of a complicated story than what I want to get into right now."

Vivian nodded. "Take all the time you need, I'm just happy to have you back. I can't believe you're back."

It wasn't till later that night that everything seemed to hit the fan. All because Lucas was annoyed with how snarky Rafe was being. Tracey informed me that it probably had something to do with Lucas having a wolf now and not understanding where he fit in the pack dynamic. There would be many challenges until he found his spot.

Rafe launched himself across the small space. "You slept in the same bed as my mate?"

Lucas grinned while he popped his knuckles.

"Yes, and you should know she only had lace and silk negligees to wear at night too."

I rolled my eyes. Why was this happening now and why was Lucas getting so much pleasure out of bothering Rafe? "Can you stop baiting him, please?"

Lucas frowned. "I don't want to stop. He just told them that they should have left me behind."

Rafe crossed his arms over his chest instead of murdering my friend. "That's because you have a thing for my mate. I can smell her all over you. It's different now."

Lucas let out an exasperated sigh. "I really don't have a thing for her."

"He's gay, remember?" Knox nudged Rafe.

"He's bi, you idiot." Rafe shook his head incredulously.

Knox made a face. "They have men that are bi?"

Tracey smacked her forehead. "Did you crawl out of the dark ages with my dad?"

He grinned at her. "Only if it gets me brownie points with him."

Lucas snarled at Knox. "Stay away from my sister."

Knox took a mocking step toward the woman in question. "What if I like them feisty?"

"Can you all just shut up?" I pinched the bridge of my nose. Idiots. But then it hit me in the face like a ton of bricks. My eyes found Rafe's. The color drained from my face. "Mate?"

Rafe took a step toward me. All of this had managed to bite him in the ass. It was written all over his face. "You weren't supposed to find out this way."

I looked between Lucas and Rafe but my words were for Lucas. "You knew? You knew and that's why you were baiting him."

Lucas's cheeks stained pink. "I might have."

Rafe snarled at him. "How did you know?"

Lucas rolled his eyes. "That first night you told me not to hurt your mate. I'm not stupid when I'm in my wolf form. Apparently ,some of you are."

Rafe didn't take that challenge. He shook his head before he looked at me. "I was going to tell you."

There was too much emotion. I struggled to breathe through it. My chest ached with the effort. I gasped as he grabbed the tops of my arms.

I had heard him but I felt like I was in a tunnel. My vision swam as I fought the realization he had given me. Nalia perked up inside my head. *Yes.* Leave it to her to wait till this moment to pop up.

I shook my head. "You did this to me. You hurt me. You changed me. Do you even know what consent means? You were a freaking creep after you hurt me."

Rafe clenched his jaw and tilted his head from side to side. "There is so much more to this than you know. I did it to save you and as far as the pursuing part afterward… sometimes my wolf doesn't get the social cues. All he wanted was to claim you, to take you, but that wasn't right. As he's calmed down, it's been easier for me to make my own decisions. I told you that."

My breathing grew rapid as I pulled my arms away from him and out of his grasp. How could he say that? I blinked a few times as it hit me. I remembered that night more clearly now and what my kidnappers had said. They had *secured Rafe Crimson's mate*. Had everyone else known but me?

I narrowed my eyes at him as I took a dangerous step toward him. "Who knows?"

I watched his throat as he swallowed and I had this odd thought to rip it out. To wrap my jaw around his neck and tear it from his shoulders. I had seen it done enough times, what was one more?

A growl rumbled up my throat. Everyone around us took a step back.

Rafe didn't move a step which was an awful thing for him. Something animalistic took over my thoughts. Nalia was purring with delight over the fact that he had admitted what she had known since she had spotted his wolf but she was also ready to defend me. She felt the pain in my chest and was ready to act on it. She was ready to tear our mate apart.

*Mate.* The word echoed around my head.

"Everyone knows."

I fought to keep control of my human form. I didn't know what would happen if I let it slip. "How long?"

"Since Tracey found out she was a witch in the woods that night." He raked his fingers through his hair. "I told them all earlier that day. I needed them to know that it wasn't a fruitless mission for someone that hadn't even pledged to the pack. They would have fought for you before, but they will die for you now. Tracey knew since she met you."

Betrayal was hot on my tongue. How could they all know? All of them but me? Was I broken? Was that why I had no idea that my mate was standing right in front of me? Weren't there supposed to be signs?

All of the familiar faces around me blurred as I took off into the woods. Anything to get away from them. Anything to not see their faces or them see mine. They had all kept it from me out of respect for their Alpha but what about respect for their friend? Their shouts followed me until Nalia ripped through my skin and we were running as one again.

## CHAPTER 58
RAFE

Everything I had planned was for nothing. I had wanted to ease her into it. I had wanted to wait and date her like I knew her human side needed. But now it was all for nothing. I would never forget the look of horror that had gone over her face. She would hate me for this. She would never forgive me. I laced my fingers behind the back of my neck and took a deep breath.

"She will be okay," Tracey patted my shoulder. What was supposed to be a good day and a great reunion had turned into a shit show.

"No, she won't be, she will never forgive me." I closed my eyes before I whipped around and stalked Lucas. I pointed my finger at him. "This is your fault."

"You have no idea what we went through in there. None at all. If you do something to me, then you're right, she won't ever forgive you. You haven't claimed her and because of that, she can walk away without pain and your wolf will go insane." Lucas pinned me with a hateful glare. "What else was I supposed to do? She would have hated me just as much if she had known I was keeping it from her too. I owe her everything. She was the only thing that gave me hope inside that hell."

I gulped. He was right. He didn't owe any of us anything. I now had to deal with the consequences of my actions. This wasn't Lucas's fault. It was mine. I should have been honest from the start and maybe all of this wouldn't have happened.

## CHAPTER 59
JADE

My body shook from fatigue as Nalia disappeared into the back of my mind again. I leaned against the door of my cottage and thankfully, it was unlocked. The door opened easily as I walked to the bathroom in-between both bedrooms. My naked body was covered in mud and leaves. I had had better days. Or better nights, judging by the sun rising now. Lucas snored from the guest bedroom and I was happy to have him here, even if he was the one that opened the can of worms. He had left the door open which gave me a comforting feeling I wasn't prepared for.

The shower was hot enough to distract me for a moment. But then it went cold and I was left with a numbness deep inside of my chest. What did I do now? I couldn't possibly go back to Rafe's house. We were mates. I had only touched the surface of what that meant. That was why Damian had wanted me. That was why he had marked me. He had known all along.

I pressed the white towel into my face and let out a silent sob. My shoulders shook with the force of it. My hands trembled as I wrapped a pink robe around my shoulders. I flipped my hair over to wrap the towel around my head. When I stood back up and opened the door Lucas was on the other side. He leaned against the wall and when he saw my face, his shoulders slumped.

"I didn't know what else to do. He had to be the one to say it." I opened my arms and he stepped into my hug immediately. He ran his hand down my back in a soothing manner. "I'm so sorry."

"There isn't anything to be sorry about, these are the things that I should have been preparing myself for. Damian kept bringing up me having a mate and I just didn't believe it or maybe, I didn't want to accept it. I don't know, either way, it is what it is."

Lucas pushed me out to arm's length. "You are the strongest person I know. If anyone can get through this, it's you. It's not going to be easy but it will be worth it. Okay?"

I managed to crack a smile. "Why does everyone keep saying that?"

Lucas smiled back. "Because it's the truth?"

"How does it feel to be accepted back into the fold?" Maybe I could take the focus off of myself for a bit. I was tired of thinking so hard. I needed a break.

Lucas's responding grin was radiant. It lit up his entire face. "The best feeling in the entire world."

Even though Tracey had invested in the best blackout curtains, I still couldn't sleep. The sun was high in the sky and it was like my body knew it. No matter what I did, sleep didn't take me. I rolled over and kicked the covers a few times before I slammed the bedroom door open then marched to the kitchen.

Lucas was sitting at the bar nursing a cup of coffee and Mav was sitting on the broken couch. He immediately hopped up to wrap me in a giant hug. My body relaxed and I smiled up at him.

"I missed you, friend."

"I missed you too, Mav." I patted his huge

shoulder and he released me. I wrinkled my nose at the coffee but dug around in the fridge for a yogurt. Judging by the grocery bags on the counter, Mav had gone grocery shopping for us. The fridge was pretty bare but it was the thought that counted. The yogurt tasted like nothing as I swallowed it down quickly. I couldn't focus on even tasting the food, my mind was too turbulent. How the heck was I going to go around the pack with all of this out in the open? How had I been so stupid?

Maybe I needed to go back home. I was stewing over that thought when Mav sat on the counter. His huge frame looked squashed up there. "What are you thinking so hard on?"

"I'm thinking I might need to go home." I nodded my head to myself. It made sense. "I can control my shifts now. I don't need to be here to protect my family."

Mav's face fell. "You don't want to be a part of this pack?"

"This pack is now my family, but I'm worried about how I am supposed to process everything that keeps happening *to* me. My control has been taken over and over again. I feel like I'm going insane. A change of pace might be nice."

"And if you have to move back to the pack, it'll

be that much harder to do so." Mav shrugged and I winced. His shoulders looked like they were ready to go a round with my cabinets.

I held my hands out with my palms up. "You should probably get down before you destroy the cabinets Tracey worked so hard on."

Lucas picked his head up from the book in his hands. "Speaking of, where is my sister?"

Mav hopped off of the counter and winced. "She's keeping Rafe busy so he doesn't come barreling in here to claim you."

I pinched the bridge of my nose. "Great, just great."

Lucas chuckled as he took a sip out of his mug. "Now that you know it's going to be harder for his wolf to not do something irrational."

"Do any of you know why he changed me against my will? You all know I'm his mate but couldn't I have been his mate while I was human?" I shook my head. None of this made sense. Just when I thought I was finally understanding the wolf dynamic/world, I was thrown for another loop.

Mav held his hands up in surrender. "I think the only one that knows is Tracey but good luck getting that out of her."

## CHAPTER 60
RAFE

Ford cast his fishing pole again and the line went soaring through the sky before it slapped the top of the water. Tracey sat behind us with a bottle of nail polish and a beer. She said it was more for the taste than anything. I wrinkled my nose. I didn't understand why anyone craved the taste of beer, but there were worse things to crave.

I shoved my hands deeper into my pockets and sighed. Ford looked at me over his shoulder. "You're thinking on it too hard."

"What do you know about any of this?" I smirked.

"I listen to mom a lot," Ford yanked on the pole and the line skipped a bit on the water. "She said she hopes that I treat my future mate with respect."

Tracey snorted behind us.

Ford ignored her. "She was really anxious when she heard about you changing Jade against her will. We had many conversations after that about what not to do when it comes to your mate. I bet if you sat down to talk to mom about it, you'd learn a lot. You just have to take your head out of your butt first."

I couldn't even help but laugh. Tracey fell into a fit of giggles. "Mother does know best."

"When will you let me talk to her?" Tracey was guarding her friend with her life. If I wanted any chance at speaking to my mate, I would have to go through her.

"When you can be honest and upfront about everything."

I rolled my eyes. "You weren't honest and upfront."

"It wasn't my secret to tell and neither are the details. You are all hell-bent on redeeming yourself. You need to start there."

**CHAPTER 61**
JADE

Granny was waiting for me in her cottage. I didn't care what Rafe had said, I needed to get this damned scar off of me and I knew the only way to do that was with magic. My boots left little indentions in the snow that Lucas followed in. I closed the door to keep the cold out. Lucas looked like he was enjoying taking his time. I wasn't going to force him to hurry for my benefit.

Carden was in the kitchen stirring something in a pot with a little blonde girl. She was talking animatedly with her hands. He said something too low for me to hear. I could have strained with my wolf senses, but I figured it was none of my business. They both laughed. The little girl flicked her hair over her shoulder and I got a peek of the side of her face. My heart stopped. Bee's daughter. She was here.

*Of course she was here.*

"She's a very gifted child. I don't think there are any with magic like hers out there." Granny said from behind me. "I am teaching her everything I know but eventually, I will have to send her to a coven. I have tried to reach out to a few but none of them want her. They said Bee was an abnormal child herself and they don't want that kind of vibe back in their covens. Poor Valentina will probably never know a family like her."

"Does she have to go to a coven?" Granny didn't have one. Maybe the child didn't need one either.

"No, Valentina doesn't need a coven but she might seek the family and bond that a coven brings. I know sometimes I miss it." Granny looked at me before she changed the subject and walked into the living area. "What can I do for you, Jade?"

"I would like you to magically remove my scar, please."

Granny's neck went taut at my suggestion. "I wish I could. But I don't think it's going to be possible. Damian used powerful magic, magic that isn't even in my jurisdiction. I could research but the archives have been closed since Damian has made such a public stance. The witches and their covens aren't looking to share their pool of knowledge with anyone unless they are from a coven. Outsiders aren't allowed."

I sighed. I had known it was a possibility that she wouldn't be able to do anything about it. But still, I had gotten my hopes up a tad. I didn't want to look at the ugly thing every day.

"Scars are apart of us, Jade. I know you don't like the way they look but they shape us into who we are. They hold powerful magic and yours probably holds more magic than any others because of who put the scar on you. Don't go about trying to get rid of it just yet. It might help us defeat the one who put it on you."

Rafe was waiting outside of Granny's home when I opened the door to leave. He was wearing a cable knit sweater and thick pants. A beanie was pulled down over his ears. He let out a breath and it formed a big cloud in front of his face.

"Hey,"

I didn't want to ignore him but I also wasn't ready to face him. "Hi,"

"I have to apologize." I stopped at his words. "I know an apology just doesn't offer much but I owe it all the same. I am so sorry. I didn't know what I was doing when I did it. I didn't know how to even tell you after the fact. When I found out you were my mate, my life changed. It stopped. I had a purpose. I had Tracey find out everything there was to know about you."

Just another lie. I knew our friendship wasn't based on truths but this made it worse. I turned away from him and began to walk away. I couldn't handle the truth. I had wanted it and now I didn't know if I could even do anything with it.

"I was horrified that my wolf would choose a human. A weak little thing like you. This girl that danced and partied. A naive girl that had no idea that monsters were stalking her mere existence." He followed behind me as he spoke. "And you didn't know life. You had no idea of a world that could give you so much. I had so much to offer. But you were a human. I could have broken you with a kiss. I could have crushed you. I didn't want to care for you. Not for one single second did I want you as my mate."

I whirled around then with murder in my eyes. "Then why do it? You could have left me alone. You could have walked away. You could have gone about your business."

"But then you caught the eye of a serial rapist." I blinked and came to a stop. "And I killed him. I saw what he had done to a girl at the previous party you have been to. I ripped him a part knowing that he would have done the same to you if I had walked away."

I should have been horrified. I should have run away from him but I didn't. I stayed right there as the snow fell from the sky and coated my lashes.

"I don't regret it either, Jade." He took a step closer to me. "I realized that night in the woods as you had to walk away from us. As you saved others. I realized that night that I would have damned the whole world if it meant you were safe but you wanted to keep the world safe. So I had to be good, I had to redeem myself. I had to try for your sake and I've been trying every day."

"All because destiny told you we were meant to be together?"

He threw his head back and looked up at the cloud-filled sky. "No, because I got to know you and your heart." He poked my chest gently. "You're stubborn. Gosh, you're so headstrong and it's not good for you or me. But the thing that really got me? How courageous you are. You weren't born into this life but somehow you grabbed it by the horns and you keep riding. You have been kicked and beaten down but not once have you given up."

"That's not true," My voice broke. "I did try to when Micah was helping me escape. I wanted to stay behind."

Rafe took a step closer and we were almost touching now. "Probably because you were trying to protect others over yourself."

I nodded. He was right.

He cupped my cheek in his hand. "I will set the world on fire and watch it burn if it means keeping *you* safe."

My heart stopped inside my chest as he leaned forward. His breath tickled my face and the scent of whiskey wrapped around me. I breathed it in deeply like my life depended on it. When his lips touched mine, all bets were off. I threw my arms around his neck and he pressed my back into the nearest tree. I could taste the truth on his tongue. He would do anything for me and I had no idea what I had done to deserve such loyalty from any man. His fingers tangled in my hair and a growl rumbled through his chest. He pulled away from me and I let out a mewling sound in the back of my throat.

He grinned. "There's no way in hell I'm claiming you up against a tree."

Knox popped his head from between the trees with a shit-eating grin. "So, when can we do karaoke again?" He scratched his chin before he spoke again. "Oh and Damian is killing witches?"

We pulled away from each other. Rafe growled. "You couldn't have started it off with that?"

Knox shrugged. "It was a burning question in my head."

I held my hands up. "How do you know?"

Knox rolled his eyes. "The kids are exploding in bright magical light. Their parent's power is getting transferred to them. At least that's what Tracey thinks."

Rafe and I looked at each other. "Shit."

Our breaths clouded out in front of us as we turned toward the manor and made a run toward all the commotion. As we ran, the sounds of screams met our ears. I winced at the sound. Rafe wrapped his fingers around mine as we broke through the tree line where chaos was erupting.

To be continued…

If you loved this book please leave a review on amazon. If you hated this book, you can leave a review too. Doesn't have to be long or sappy, just something simple. Reviews help authors make a living. Thanks!

**NOTE FROM THE AUTHOR**

If you loved Tracey's POV, look for her novel coming in early 2022.

## ACKNOWLEDGMENTS

Another day, another thank you page. Wow. This book was probably written faster than any of my other's besides my military romances. This story needed to be told more than any other story I have ever written. It's so weird how that happens. As I was writing this story, I thought of my own redemption that I had to go through. I hope you know you are never too far gone for love or acceptance. You are never too bad or worthless. You are worthy, even if you don't think you are. Your worth was determined thousands if not hundreds of thousands of years ago. *You are loved. You are redeemable. You are worthy.*

Thank you so much, first to my mother. My mother never gets enough credit for things she has done for me and my family but also for me as the child and the teenager. I told y'all in Take Me that the book was for my past self. My mother always saw good in me. She always wanted the best for me. She still does. She was the one that taught me about redemption and forgiveness. Without her I wouldn't be the person I am TODAY. Thank you, mom, you raised a pretty bad ass chick if I do as so myself ;)

Next I have to thank my husband because somedays I holed myself up in my office all day and got absolutely nothing done but then he would come home and take care of laundry or make dinner. I don't always express my gratitude eloquently enough but thank you for helping me. Thank you for being here for me. Thank you for being my person.

Thank you to my Mason, my little goober, I hope someday you read these and know how much I love you. I love listening to you play pretend in the other room. Some days when Im having a brain fart, you help give me a break with different words to use. Thank you for having such a wild imagination. Thank you for sharing it with me.

Thank you to my fabulous editor that listens to my voice messages and rambling almost everyday and just goes with it. I couldn't have done any of this without you. Brittany, you are a gem, don't ever let anyone tell you differently. Thank you for being one of my people! Also… thank you to your husband Alister, his words of advice and encouragement are always a breath of fresh air. I'll never get tired of your perfect family. I adore y'all.

Thank you to my friends Tori and Allison, that give me plenty of amazing *friend* material to write about. I don't think I would be able to write such great supporting characters without the both fo you in my corner.

Thank you to all of you readers that fell in love with my characters and have stayed for the long haul. I know I write super fast but y'all keep devouring them. As long as you love them, I'll keep writing them. Thank you for supporting me.

**ALSO BY A. LONERGAN**

*Witches of Jackson Square series-*

Transfixed

Fixated

Captivated

Enraptured

*Tales from the Mirror Realm-*

Assassin's Reign

Assassin's Liege

Assassin's Will

*Kingdoms and Curses-*

Ashes to Ashes

Beasts and Beauty

*Brothers Bound series-*

Euphoria

Nostalgia

A. Lonergan's life wasn't always a happily ever after, because of this she knows that sometimes the best stories aren't. She knows that sometimes real life comes with grit and darkness, so her stories do too. She loves to read anything and everything she can get her hands on but she has a soft spot for fantasy.

*She lives in southern Louisiana where the food is full of comfort, the people like their tea sweet, and the stories are full of soul.*

Printed in Great Britain
by Amazon